An Affair of Love

by
S. Anne Gardner

AN AFFAIR OF LOVE
© 2008 BY S. ANNE GARDNER

ISBN 10: 1-933113-86-3
ISBN 13: 978-1-933113-86-9

First Printing: 2008

This Trade Paperback Is Published By
Intaglio Publications
Walker, LA
WWW.INTAGLIOPUB.COM

CREDITS
EXECUTIVE EDITOR: TARA YOUNG
COVER DESIGN BY SHERI

DEDICATION

Mujer bella de mi vida...regalame un beso, amame con locura, llena mis brazos con el calor de ti....

ACKNOWLEDGMENTS

This page is often overlooked, yet in this page, we see how the author gets this far and the product is made possible. Without all these incredible people in my life, this book would never have been written nor would it have been published. Thank you to each and every one of you.

To the woman who holds my heart: I acknowledge your existence, and I thank you for teaching me what love is. Thank you for showing me that in spite it all, somehow love thrives and endures even beyond the impossible.

To my boys, the most precious loves of my life, you make everything beautiful. You fill my life with so much wonder. I cannot imagine—nor would I desire—a life without you.

Alina, my oldest and dearest friend, my life since I met you, at the mere age of twelve, became all the better. I cannot imagine living without you. You are more than friend, you are my family. I could not have desired nor do I deserve a sister as supportive as you have been my whole life. It is true we are born into a family, but the one who cries with us and lives the every day, we create. Words have never been necessary between us, but I have the need to express them at this time in my life. In the best and in the worst of times, your love and your friendship I have never doubted. I love you with my whole heart.

Angel, you have been more than friend. In the darkest time of my life, you were there, and I know that I am alive because of you. I don't deserve you, but I am so grateful for the gift of you in my life. When all closed in around me and I felt the searing pain that brought me to my knees, you, Angel, kept the hordes at bay and took me somewhere safe so that I might heal and prepare to fight again. My arm will always be yours and my allegiance a promise that will only end upon my death. Dear Angel, my dear and true friend, how I do love you.

Belinda, how can I thank you for listening day and night? How can I ever tell you how significant and wonderful it is to have you in my life? You have shown me that friendship lasts and that it is rare. I know that you are so much a part of my life I could not imagine one second without you. I share so much with you, and it is in the little things that the every day is made special. My dearest friend, I love you.

Char, how can I thank you for the truth that you always give me, even when I don't want to hear it? Your friendship is one that I will treasure for many years to come. Thank you for all the listening, thank you for your eternal support. Thank you for the late hours of the night that you were a real friend to me. I will always remember, and I will always love you for this and for so much more.

Grace, thank you for constantly calling and always caring to know that I am okay. In the insanity of this world, I know that I can reach out to you and you will always be there. Don't change, Grace, you are truly special. And yes, I love you, too.

Marie, words will never be enough. You will always be a part of my life as you have always been. You hang on to me because. I will always be by your side whenever you need me. My dearest Marie, I will always be there for all the years to come because there will be many. You showed me how special life is…and what a gift it is to have one more day. Thank you for being there. I will never be able to thank you enough. I love you my friend.

Joey, my thanks go out to you, as well, my dear friend. I know that no matter what happens in life, you will always be there to tell me it's going to be okay. Somehow you always see the best in me; how I do love you for that. Thank you for believing when I could not.

To Tara, my editor, who patiently nudges me along. Thank you so much for the patience. You have made this story so much better with your input. You have been great to work with. You made it all seem painless; I know I tried your patience. Thank you for hanging in there with me.

Robin/Sheri, thank you for listening and for the friendship. Thank you for this book. It has been a real privilege to know you and to work with you.

And my very special thanks to all my Gems….you are a constant and a real positive input in all my writing. Thank you to all of you for the patience to wait for an update and for the supportive e-mails. This book is also very much a part of all of you.

Chapter One

"You can't be serious," Blayne said, expressing her frustration at the old man.

"I'm very serious," he said. Arthur Aston-Carlyle looked tired. He sat down behind his desk and waved for her to sit on one of the chairs near her.

"Does Mother know?" Blayne decided to try another argument.

"Abigail and I spoke last night," he said. "She knows what I want to do."

"Arthur…how can you be sure?" Blayne had known and loved him long enough to know that there was no deterring the man from the course he had chosen, and he knew that when she referred to him as Arthur, she was trying to think rationally rather than letting her emotions interfere.

"Be sure?" He didn't understand her question.

"That this woman is indeed your child," Blayne clarified.

"I know."

"Then why…?"

"Why didn't I ever recognize my own daughter?"

"Well, yes, Arthur, why didn't you?" Blayne got up and paced the room, trying to control her anger.

"I was young—"

"Bullshit!" Blayne walked toward the desk and hit it with her fist. "Jesus, you left them in the middle of a civil

1

war." She never broke eye contact with the man who until that afternoon she had respected. "You just walked away, leaving them to face it all."

"You never did let me get away with anything," Arthur said proudly.

She suddenly seemed deflated and sat back down in one of the chairs in front of his desk.

"How do you know she'll want to meet you?"

"Because I want to meet her," he said arrogantly.

Blayne looked up and smiled for a moment before becoming serious again. "Jesus, Dad, you are one for surprises."

"I've always counted on you Blayne. That's why I need you to do this."

"What makes you think that…?" She was visibly confused, but suddenly, something akin to understanding covered her face. No! She couldn't believe what had just occurred to her. "She doesn't know, does she?" Blayne stood up again.

"No, she doesn't." Arthur didn't blink.

Blayne ran her fingers through her hair. "You think she would turn you away, your daughter, I mean? What makes you think she won't do the same with me?"

"Because no one has ever been able to say no to you." Arthur smiled.

"No, this is something you're going to have to do, Arthur. No." Blayne felt the anger coming up her throat. "I can't believe all this!"

"I'm dying, Blayne."

She stared at him in shock. It was just like Arthur to blurt out things like this. She should have known from the beginning that there wasn't to be a choice.

"What are you talking about?"

"I have pancreatic cancer, I'm dying. I want to make

things right. I need you to do this for me."

"Damn you, Arthur! Damn you!" Blayne yelled as she grabbed the file and stormed out of the library.

Arthur sat back on his chair and closed his eyes. He had never doubted that Blayne would do this for him. What he did regret, however, was having told her about his illness in that fashion. Opening his eyes, he stared at the door and again regretted how he had handled things.

Arthur Aston-Carlyle had married Abigail Anberville thirty-three years earlier. Two years later, they had a daughter they named Diana. Diana was the opposite of Blayne. Where Blayne had always been responsible, Diana was not. Blayne was a star athlete and an honors student. Diana barely scraped by. Diana seemed to have only one desire, and that was to have a good time. Blayne had always been protective of her sister, and Diana relied on that love to get her out of more than one mess.

Blayne was barely four when Arthur married Abigail. Her brother Charles, who they all called Chaz, was seven at the time. Arthur loved them as his own. But Blayne was the one he favored because of her vitality and her desire to excel, and in return, she had made him proud.

She had passion in everything; however, she had never found anyone to share her life with. She was too busy doing, and after a while, even Abigail said she thought Blayne was incapable of loving anyone with her whole heart.

Chaz didn't seem to have the desire to settle down in the near future, either. There were rumors here and there about his affairs, but nothing ever materialized as a result of them. He was in his late thirties with no future to speak of. He was happy just spending money and flying from one hot spot to another. The truth was that Chaz was a disappointment. He had hurt his mother too many times, and as much as Arthur loved him, he decided that he had to think of the future.

Diana was heading in the same direction. Arthur hoped that Blayne would settle down and give him grandchildren, but that had not happened, either. Abigail had been right—Blayne just didn't seem interested in a personal life. She didn't seem to need anyone. And he had to admit, he wanted to see his progeny before he died.

Arthur hadn't thought of Elena Agramonte in years. When he was told of his illness, he realized that he had another child he'd never seen and might never see. It became very important to him to find Elena.

A few months before, he had asked his attorneys to make inquiries. Three days earlier, he got the call. Elena had married the local playboy Humberto Sotomayor and had raised their daughter as her husband's child. A daughter. He had a daughter. He remembered when he got the photos of his child. She had grown to be a beautiful woman. She had her mother's lustrous hair, but there were also signs of him in her skin color and eyes.

Gabriella Matheson, as his daughter was now called, was a beautiful woman. Her hair was the color of rich sable, and thick dark lashes framed her eyes, which were the blue of a tumultuous sky, much like his own. There was so much of Elena in her. Something inside him grew warm. Elena had given him a child, and Arthur felt the pangs of regret yet again.

Gabriella was married and had two children. When he saw the photograph of his grandchildren, he knew he had to meet her. He had loved Elena, but he had been too young and too arrogant to think beyond what he wanted at the time. Arthur knew his parents would never accept a girl from an island in the Caribbean. Elena did not come from money. And his family was incredibly wealthy.

Elena had been beautiful and kind. She had believed his words of love and his promises of a tomorrow. When he left her, he knew it would break her heart. Blayne was right; he had simply walked away and left her to fend for herself. He did try to make inquiries when the civil war escalated in Cuba, but after a while, he didn't even try to find out anything else. He had simply turned the page and put her out of his mind. He should have stayed and married her, he told himself. How different things might have been if he had. Even in that thought, he recognized his selfishness.

Arthur had to admit that he loved Abigail. She had come from a good family, so it had been a good addition to his family tree. His parents had been happy at his choice of wife, and in turn, he was given a generous income. Abigail had been a young widow when he met her. Her husband, Brian, had been killed in car accident a year earlier. For a few years, he played the faithful husband. When Diana was born, he had been truly happy. Then as the years went by, the children became such a disappointment. All had disappointed him one way or another— except for Blayne.

She was so much his child, but there was something about her that he could never quite understand and that disturbed him. She was brilliant and proud, but there was a flaw in her. Blayne's beauty was arresting. People turned their heads when she entered a room, yet no one ever caught her eye. Blayne loved him; he knew that. But Blayne didn't need or want anyone to share her life with.

Arthur had once tried talking to her about her private life. She only told him to mind his own business. Arthur remembered he had laughed. Blayne should have been his child. Blayne should have been...the son he'd always wanted. She was resolute and aloof. She was in control of her life, and she never wavered from the course she set for herself. She was now running most of his businesses. She was ruthless, but she was also loyal. Where he would never have trusted Chaz or even his own daughter Diana with this power, he had trusted Blayne.

Blayne was his daughter as much as Abigail's, he told himself. He had raised her. She was as stubborn and arrogant as he was, and for that, she was close to his heart. She was too much like him, he realized, and that saddened him. Like him, she would make many mistakes. He only hoped that she would not be filled with regret at the end of her life, as well.

Blayne sat behind her desk. She'd been sitting there for hours now. Arthur was dying. And now she had to get a complete stranger to agree to see him.

Standing, Blayne walked toward the huge glass window. Her office was on the twenty-fifth floor of the Aston-Carlyle Building. Arthur was a sanctimonious, self-absorbed son of a bitch, and the only father she'd ever known. Ever since she could remember, he had been there. So many times, she told herself that one day she would be able to truly talk to him about her life. Blayne always thought there would be a tomorrow, but tomorrow was here and he would never know her.

She walked back to her desk, sat down, and opened the file before her. She read the report and went over all the documentation the attorneys had provided. Short of a DNA test, all signs showed that Gabriella Matheson was indeed Arthur's daughter. All the dates and facts pointed toward that. Blayne ran her fingers through her hair. She felt drained. She leaned back in her chair, letting her head fall back.

"Damn you, Arthur. Damn you. You knew I was going to do this, didn't you, you old man?" Blayne said with a sad smile. "Too used to getting your way."

She finished reading the rest of the report about Gabriella. She had married Joseph Matheson when she was twenty. Three years later, her daughter Elena was born, and two years after that, she had a son named Christopher. Joseph was a prominent attorney and Gabriella was a homemaker.

Gabriella had gone to college the last few years and finished her degree in art history. She was an artist. Blayne leaned back for a moment. Somehow this surprised her. Arthur's daughter was an artist. Gabriella was a sculptor.

Blayne opened the yellow envelopes and pulled out the photos the attorneys had provided. She saw a few pictures of the children. And then she saw a picture of whom she thought was Joseph Matheson. She turned the photo over to confirm it. Then she saw the face of Gabriella. Blayne stared at the photograph in silence.

"She looks like an artist," Blayne said out loud.

"And what does an artist look like?"

Blayne looked up to see her mother come into the room.

"Mother, I didn't know you were—"

"I knew you'd be here. Did he talk to you?" Abigail asked.

"Yes." Blayne seemed embarrassed.

Abigail stared at her daughter for a moment. Blayne always surprised her somehow. She was embarrassed for her, Abigail realized.

"It's all right, Blayne. May I see the photo?" Abigail asked as her hand went out.

Blayne gave her the photo of Gabriella.

"She's very beautiful," Abigail said. "Do you also have a photo of her mother?"

Blayne looked at the rest of the photos and handed another photo to her mother.

"Yes" was all Abigail said as she handed Blayne the photos back.

"He wants me to get this woman Gabriella Matheson to see him," Blayne said. She took back the photo from her mother and looked at it.

"We spoke last night. What do you think? Is it possible?"

"Mother, short of a DNA test..."

"What does your analytical mind tell you?" Abigail pulled no punches.

"I would say that everything points to her being Arthur's daughter."

Abigail closed her eyes.

"I'm sorry, Mother. I don't know why you're surprised. Arthur has always been...I'm surprised this hasn't happened before," Blayne said coldly.

"I should divorce him."

"Don't be ridiculous. Let's not go into this again. Let's skip the drama and get down to business, okay? You know you're not going to divorce him. Is it true?" Blayne was aggravated by her mother's attitude. After every argument between her and Arthur, she said the same thing.

"Is what true?"

"That he has pancreatic cancer?" Blayne waited for what seemed like a lifetime.

"Mother?"

"Yes, it's true." Abigail suddenly looked old. "I do love him, you know."

"I know you do."

"Do you? Do you think he knows that?" Abigail's eyes filled with tears. "I often wonder if he knows."

"I'm sure he knows." Blayne tried to sound reassuring.

"He's been a difficult man to love. I never really know what he's thinking. I doubt he'll ever know that I really did marry him because I loved him."

Blayne was surprised at this confession. She'd never seen her mother like this. It was true then. Arthur *was* dying. And here was her mother saying things she never thought she would hear. And yes, she was surprised. She loved Arthur. Why did it surprise her so much? Why should it surprise her that her mother loved him?

"No one ever thought I did. They all thought I married him for the money."

Blayne looked back at her without saying a word.

"He was so handsome. I fell in love at first sight." Abigail smiled wistfully. "Our first night together, he said her name in his sleep." Tears ran down her face.

Blayne remained quite.

"It broke my heart. I never said a word to him. I knew even then that he loved someone else. But you can't control who you love, can you?" Abigail looked at her pitifully.

Blayne didn't know what to say. Her mother had known all these years. Knowing that her mother knew somehow hurt her inside.

"I'm sorry."

"And now he's dying. What will I do without him?" Abigail looked into her daughter's eyes. "The girl is very beautiful."

"Yes, she is."

Blayne walked to the front door and rang the doorbell. A moment later, the door opened and in front of her stood Gabriella. *The photos did not do her justice*, Blayne thought. She stared at the woman for a moment before snapping out of her trance.

"Yes? May I help you?"

"My name is Blayne Anberville. I need to speak to you."

Gabriella noticed that the woman in front of her was incredibly beautiful. She was impeccably dressed, and Gabriella could see the black limousine parked in her driveway.

"And who are you?" Gabriella smiled, a little intrigued.

"My name is Blayne…"

Gabriella laughed. Blayne saw the beautiful face light up, and all she could do was stare again. *Such a lovely sound*, Blayne thought as she smiled a little back. "I know that part," Gabriella said playfully.

"I'm here representing Arthur Aston-Carlyle," Blayne said quickly, feeling awkward for the first time in her life.

Gabriella smiled at the frazzled woman in front of her. For some reason, this woman was acting like her daughter when she had done something naughty. She decided to take pity on the beautiful stranger.

"I'm sorry, I don't know who that is. Are you sure you have the right house?"

"You are Gabriella Matheson. I have the right house and the right person." Blayne inwardly chastised herself for letting a beautiful woman's smile shake her to her foundation. "As I was saying, Mrs. Matheson, I represent Arthur Aston-Carlyle, your father."

The smile was gone from the lovely face in front of her and Blayne felt cold.

"I think you have the wrong person. My father's name is Humberto Sotomayor."

"No, Mrs. Matheson, it's not," Blayne insisted. "I know this is probably not the best way to find out about this, but time is of the—" Blayne noticed that the other woman grew pale.

"I can explain all this to you if you give me a few minutes." Blayne took a step closer to Gabriella, who searched her eyes in desperation. The confusion Blayne saw troubled her because she was the one who had put it there. "You have your father's eyes," Blayne said out of nowhere. "His are the same shade of blue."

Gabriella took a step back and Blayne walked in. She

took a few steps inside, then turned toward Gabriella, who was still standing in a daze by the door.

Gabriella looked at her and Blayne was taken aback when she saw the pain in her eyes as they filled with tears. "My eyes...?"

"Yes, you have his eyes," Blayne said gently. Somehow she knew that had hit home. In her need to rush through this task, she saw the pain she was causing. A perfectly happy woman had opened the door, and the same woman now seemed forlorn.

Gabriella passed by her, picked up a phone, and dialed. Blayne came up behind her and took it away from her. Gabriella faced her as tears ran down her face. "Give that back to me!"

Blayne hung up the receiver. "Let me talk to you first."

"No, I need to talk to my mother."

"I don't think that's such a good idea."

"I bet you don't." Gabriella sounded angry now.

Blayne took a step back; she would let things take their course. Gabriella picked up the phone and dialed, facing Blayne all the while.

"Mama...Mama, I need to talk to you. I need to ask you something...No, I'm okay." Gabriella took a deep breath, never breaking eye contact with Blayne. "Who is Arthur Aston-Carlyle?"

Blayne saw the moment it happened. Blayne saw the beautiful woman's heart break into a million pieces in front of her. It was clear in Gabriella's eyes, and she had been the one to bring her the news.

Gabriella hung up the phone without a word. She trembled, and Blayne did something that both women would later remember and question. Blayne took Gabriella into her arms as the other woman sobbed loudly, clinging to the warm arms that surrounded her.

"My eyes…always my eyes," Gabriella said as she wept. Her body shook with the sobbing and Blayne held her tighter. Gabriella's whole body was pressed against her; she was clinging to Blayne inconsolably as an old pain had been brought to light and cruelly exposed.

Blayne caressed the soft hair and kissed the woman's head. She pulled Gabriella even tighter to her. All that the world seemed to hold for Blayne at that moment was the softness of the woman in her arms.

Gabriella wanted the world to open up and swallow her whole. Her eyes had always been the subject of snickers and suppositions. That same topic had been a sensitive subject and an argument between her parents ever since she could remember. Her father had died over ten years before, and at the end, they had been close. She treasured those last months and she hated her blue eyes, which everyone found necessary to mention. As a child, schoolteachers even expressed interest when her parents would attend parent-teacher conferences. After a while, her father just didn't go anymore. He began to look at her differently. He never said a word to her. He loved her…she was his child, but Gabriella felt the distance between them.

"He must have known. My father must have known." Gabriella sobbed as she buried herself in the warmth of the arms around her.

"Shh…it's all right. Shh…" Blayne said as her hands caressed Gabriella's back.

Gabriella only felt the strength of Blayne's arms. It had been so long since she'd felt the security of such an embrace. Only in her father's arms had she ever felt as safe as she did now, and she gave herself to that emotion she so desperately needed. She leaned into Blayne and cried all the harder.

Her father had been gone for so long. Her husband had stopped making her feel anything similar to safety for a long time. Gabriella clung to the security of the arms that held her so tightly; after a while, all she felt was the heat in her body begin to burn and encompass her. She clung to that warmth and sought it.

The world became filled with strong arms and soft caresses as she looked up to meet lips that covered her own. Blayne's eyes closed and the emptiness that had always been inside her suddenly filled. She had felt the cold inside her grow for so long, and now Gabriella pressed harder against her, which seemed to cover her body with the warmth she had sought her whole life.

Blayne wasn't sure how it happened. One moment all she could do was kiss the soft dark tresses of hair. Then Gabriella's mouth came up and her mouth naturally met it. There was no thinking. Suddenly, her thoroughly orderly life crashed around her, and for the first time, she didn't care about anything. Blayne didn't think; she didn't weigh her actions or her options as she did with every other step and action in her life. Something inside her, long dormant, had taken over, and the emotion was all that mattered.

Passion was the only thing that seemed to reign, where they were did not matter, who they were was not important. They had no will. The desire had awakened, and it would not be denied. Hands traveled and explored as mouths tasted and bit hungrily. There were no expectations, no questions. Each woman could no more fight what was happening than she could continue living without taking another breath.

Blayne's hands unbuttoned Gabriella's blouse of their own accord before Gabriella realized Blayne's mouth was sucking hungrily on her breast. Gabriella's head fell back in wanton abandonment as a moan escaped her lips.

A car door slammed. Something in Blayne's head clicked through her jumbled emotions, and she pulled away quickly but not before locking gazes with those of the woman who had made her lose all control. Gabriella cried a little as she tried to pull Blayne back toward her.

"Someone just got here," Blayne said, trying to catch her breath. Holding Gabriella's hand tightly, she took a few long steps to the door and locked it moments before the knob turned. That one action would give them the minute they both needed.

Gabriella's hands were trembling as she tried to button her blouse. Blayne pushed her hands away and finished the task for her. Blayne then looked up into those blue eyes again and saw the distance growing between them. She pulled Gabriella roughly into her arms once more and kissed her soundly and hungrily on the lips. Both women just regarded each other questioning, waiting, guessing...until the pounding on the door shook them out of their trance.

Blayne took a few steps away and waited for an even more distressed Gabriella to open the door.

Gabriella stared at her a moment longer, then suddenly, she seemed to realize the enormity of what had just happened.

The knocking grew louder still.

"You better open the door, Mrs. Matheson," Blayne said coldly.

That was all Gabriella needed. Her blood that had a moment ago been boiling had turned cold as she felt the frigidity of the iceberg before her.

Gabriella turned and opened the door. Her mother came in looking distraught.

Elena Sotomayor walked in and noticed the other woman in the room. She quickly deduced that said woman was the one who had given her daughter the news. Elena was not sure what or how much her daughter knew, so she would wait and listen before she said anything.

"Mama..." Gabriella's hands trembled. She could not

look at her mother, and she wanted to hide from Blayne. What had just happened? Her whole life had just changed forever. It would never be the same again.

"What's wrong, Leila?" Elena asked, using her pet name for her daughter. Gabriella looked up with pained, tear-filled eyes.

"Mama...tell me. I want you to tell me," Gabriella begged.

Elena's eyes filled with tears, as well. Gabriella shook her head and put her arms around her body as she took a few steps away from her mother.

"Is it true, Mama? Is it true?" Gabriella waited. When Elena looked up, she knew.

"Leila—"

"Did Papa know?"

"No."

Gabriella walked over to the couch and sat down. Blayne asked herself how she ever thought she could just make this happen and...she had not thought, she admitted to herself. She had made cold calculations. She had not factored in any of her own emotions, but in retrospect, she should have. That perhaps was the problem. Blayne was coldly processing as Elena Sotomayor now faced her.

"You, you told my daughter this news?"

"I represent Arthur Aston-Carlyle. Yes, I told her. He sent me to bring her to him." Blayne figured she should just put it all out there and see what happened. Damage control was something she had always been good at.

"Bring her to him?" Elena asked in indignation.

"My father is dying. He wants to see her before he passes." Blayne saw the shock of the news register in the older woman's face. *Interesting,* Blayne thought.

Gabriella got up and faced Blayne in horror. "Your father?" Gabriella looked like she was going to be sick.

15

"Mama—"

Elena went to her daughter immediately and helped her sit down again. Gabriella then fainted.

"Leila?" Elena looked like she was going to pass out, as well.

"She's fainted. Please get a wet towel and some cold water for her to drink." Blayne took control of the situation. Elena looked down at her daughter, who seemed to be between consciousness and unconsciousness

"She's had a shock. Please get the water, Mrs. Sotomayor. I'll stay with her," Blayne said as she sat next to Gabriella on the sofa.

Elena got up on shaky legs and walked out of the room.

Blayne pulled the semiconscious Gabriella toward her. She caressed the face of the woman in her arms. Gabriella's eyes fluttered open. Their gazes once again locked.

"No," Gabriella cried as she pulled away. "You knew? And you?" Gabriella seemed mortified with the implications of the news. *If all this is true, Blayne is my half sister!* She began to pale again. *Oh, my God! Oh, my God!*

"Are you better now?" Blayne asked her politely, totally ignoring the accusation in Gabriella's eyes. "Arthur married my mother when I was four years old."

Gabriella raised a shaky hand to her temple, trying to catch her breath. At that moment, Elena came into the room with the towel and the glass of water. Blayne got up and took them from her.

"Here, drink this." Blayne placed the tip of the glass at Gabriella's mouth. She then put the glass down and wiped her face gently with the moist towel. "I know that this has been…a day full of surprises." Blayne noticed the slight cringe. "As I said, Arthur is dying and wants to meet you. That's all."

Elena beheld her daughter, unable to say anything.

Gabriella looked at her mother with so many questions.

"Leila…" Elena said full of emotion as she sat across from her daughter.

"Arthur abandoned your mother. He left her with very little choices. He just found out he's dying and wants to meet you, his daughter." Blayne laid it all out for them. There was no point in playing with the truth. And by addressing it, she might be able to assist Elena in explaining her actions to Gabriella.

"He was a young man who arrogantly only thought of himself. He made a terrible mistake…and it cost him. He wants to meet you, and I'm here to take you to him," Blayne said.

Elena was still silent. Gabriella looked toward her mother, who seemed distraught. "Mother?"

"I'm sorry, Leila. I'm so sorry." Elena covered her face. "I never wanted you to know."

"Arthur told me how badly he behaved toward you. I'm sorry, Mrs. Sotomayor," Blayne said. "I left my mother in tears, as well."

Gabriella now looked toward Blayne and got up. "No."

"No?" Blayne did not understand.

"I'm not going," Gabrielle said as she faced Blayne and dared her to challenge her. "No."

"You're upset. I'll come back tomor—"

"Didn't you hear what I said? No!" Gabrielle yelled.

Elena went to her daughter's side.

"Get out!" Gabriella demanded.

Blayne stood and challenged her with her eyes. Suddenly, she smiled. "I'll come back. And you won't be able to say no to me…again." Blayne let the double entendre float between them. When she saw the shock of understanding register in Gabriella's eyes, she knew she had won.

Blayne walked into her penthouse in Boston a few hours later and went straight to her office to get ready for a dinner meeting. She had taken the shuttle from Princeton, New Jersey, to Boston, Massachusetts. Blayne had a full schedule and had planned other meetings around her visit to Gabriella Matheson. She had factored in the possibility that there might be some reservations on Gabriella's part.

What had completely thrown her for a loop was Gabriella herself. Never in her wildest dreams could she have imagined what had happened between them. She still could not bring herself to believe it. Blayne then called her office and instructed her secretary to reschedule all her appointments for the next few days. She would fly back to Princeton first thing in the morning. Gabriella Matheson had suddenly become her number one priority.

Chapter Two

The children were already asleep when Gabriella spoke to Joseph on the phone. He was away on business and would be back in a few days. He asked the usual questions; they seemed to be polite strangers these days unless they were arguing. She said nothing to him about what had happened that day. After all, she told herself, it was family business. At that moment, she realized that her marriage was over. It had slowly but surely died.

Gabriella walked around the house in the dark dazed. She remembered how in the beginning she had put so much of herself into making her house a home. What a disappointment her marriage had been. Even in the beginning, she should have known.

From almost the first day of their marriage, something began to dissolve between them. It was as if after the moment she gave herself to Joseph, something inside her rejected him. It wasn't something she could put her finger on, but it was there, and it grew until she could hardly breathe.

In retrospect, she realized that she had bestowed qualities on Joseph that he had never possessed. She had always seen more than there had been. Gabriella had to admit feeling a great sadness. The truth was that she had been more in love with love than with Joseph.

They had both been young. He was handsome and outgoing. Joseph had been attentive and romantic early in their relationship until it began to dissipate.

After the first two years, she could see the cracks. They slowly but surely began to live their own lives. They had actually separated twice within that following year. She would leave, and he would call her parents, who would advise her to return to her husband. In the end, she would cave in and go back. The last time, she realized she would not leave again unless it was going to be final. Just thinking that thought should have made her situation more than clear.

So many times after that, she had wanted to leave but had not. It was better that she stayed for the children's sake, she told herself. The children had been the reason she had not changed anything. Her father would tell her over and over again: *A child needs their father, Leila. Don't take their father away from them. Joseph is a good husband to you. He is a good provider.* She always gave in after that. Only now did she realize that she had stayed out of some sense of guilt because of her father. Is that how he had seen things through his eyes? Did he use the same argument with her mother? Did he know about her?

Gabriella's tormented mind cried out. She walked toward her studio. There she would find peace. She had always poured her passion into her art. She sculpted with all the emotions that filled her and needed to get out somehow. She had never found another human being to share that place deep inside her that she alone entered. In her work, Gabriella lived and loved. In the sculptured shapes of clay lay her life with a promise but still unfinished.

A critic had said her work was created of something raw and a sensuality that begged to be born. After that particular critique, her work was highly sought after. Gabriella went into her studio and began to mold the clay and envision its outcome. Her hands took on a life of their own and the clay came alive.

"How did it go?" a voice said on the phone.

"Hello and good evening to you, too, Arthur," Blayne said sarcastically.

"How did it go, Blayne?"

"What did you expect? She didn't take it well, that's for sure." Blayne sat on the bed.

"Will she come?" He tried to hide the anxiety in his voice.

Blayne took a deep breath. "She said she wants nothing to do with you. That's how things stand right now." Blayne ran her fingers through her hair. "I'll go back tomorrow to discuss it with her again."

"Blayne, I...I would like to see her before..." The silence became palpable between them.

"I don't think I handled things well, Arthur... perhaps..."

"If anyone can do this, it's you," Arthur said reassuringly.

"We...kind of clashed. Perhaps Chaz or Diana can talk to—"

"No, you're the one. Blayne, you can make someone in the desert want to buy sand," Arthur said humorously.

"It's just that...this is not business, and she's your daughter," Blayne justified her reluctance.

"Emphasize the idea of family. From her file, I can see she values that. Appeal to her obligation, she is an only child. She might want to get to know her other siblings."

"Arthur, I don't know..."

"Advise her like a sister..."

"I am not her sister!"

Arthur said nothing for a moment. Blayne had surprised him with her declaration. She was usually so in control of things; this type of outburst was out of character for her.

S. Anne Gardner

"You are as much my daughter as she and Diana are."

Blayne remained silent. How could she tell him she believed him if the thought of Gabriella being her sister made her feel ill. That would never happen, she told herself.

"Blayne...?"

"I'll try again tomorrow."

"Good, I knew I could count on you. Keep me apprised. Good night."

"Good night, Father," Blayne said to appease his ruffled feathers. Arthur had been a father to her. She owed him this. Somehow she would make Gabriella go to him.

After terminating the call, Blayne just stared in front of her. What had possessed her to kiss Gabriella? She had always been so careful about hiding who and what she was. How could she have done such an utterly irresponsible thing? And now she had to go back and somehow convince this woman to see someone who had abandoned her.

Blayne reasoned that in the past she had often come upon people who had not wanted to see things her way, and she had known how to deal with them. She would make Gabriella Matheson see things her way. Everyone had a weak spot, Blayne had learned from Arthur, and she always found it. But this was different. Gabriella was Arthur's daughter. And whether she wanted to admit it or not, Blayne had kissed her. Why? Why had she done something as insane as that?

Neither woman found much sleep that night, and when they did, all she found was the haunting memory of one kiss playing itself over and over again.

Gabriella woke up late, starting her morning off badly. The children missed the bus, so she had to drive them to school. The phone was ringing when she walked into the house. She ran to pick it up, but the line was dead by then.

"Shit!"

22

She walked back and closed the front door. The phone rang again.

"Hello?"

"Leila?"

"Yes, Mom."

"Where were you?"

"The kids missed the bus. I took them to school."

"Are you okay?"

"I…I'm okay, Mama." Gabriella tried to control her emotions.

"Can you come over for lunch?"

"No…I'm working on a piece and I…um, I need to work on it." Gabriella needed the distance.

"All right, I'll call you later then," Elena said sadly.

"Mama…."

The doorbell rang and Gabriella walked over to answer it while talking to her mother on the cordless phone.

"Mama, I just need to think—" She opened the door and came face to face with Blayne. Gabriella's mouth opened in surprise. She could feel her pulse quicken almost immediately. Gabriella heard her mother call her name over and over again.

"Leila? Leila? Are you all right?"

Blayne walked right in.

"Um…yes, Mama, I'm okay. I'll call you later." Gabriella terminated the call and turned toward Blayne, leaving the front door open.

"Please go, we have nothing else to discuss. I'm not going anywhere!"

Blayne turned quickly and was in front of her. She reached out and Gabriella gasped as she felt herself being pushed against the door. Apparently, Blayne's intent was to close the door, but they were now standing very close to each other.

Their faces were mere inches apart. Blayne breathed deeply, and the emotions that became uncontrollable every time she got close to Gabriella surfaced with the speed of a running train. She looked down at Gabriella's mouth, then up to her eyes again.

Gabriella wanted to speak, yet nothing was coming out of her mouth. She could hear heavy pounding in her ears that threatened to overwhelm her.

Blayne was leaning in when the phone that Gabriella was holding began to ring and ring.

"Your phone," Blayne said softly.

Gabriella searched her eyes, seeming not to understand. The phone continued to ring as Blayne leaned in to kiss her.

"No," Gabriella said, and Blayne stopped. Their mouths were so close they almost touched. A whimper escaped Gabriella as Blayne's mouth covered hers hungrily.

Again, it was like a ball of fire seemed to be consuming them. There was no coherent thought as both women melted into each other. Their bodies fused in a primal need to connect. Blayne's mouth traveled down Gabriella's neck hungrily as she moaned. As soon as she felt Blayne's hand begin to undo her blouse, she pushed her away hard.

"No!" Gabriella said as she leaned against the door for support. Blayne stood in front of her, trying to catch her breath. She was staring at Gabriella as if she had been betrayed. Gabriella now stared at her as if she had been the one that should apologize. For an instant, she saw betrayal written clearly in those eyes that were now coldly looking back at her. The passion was gone, and Gabriella could physically feel the cold emanating from Blayne.

Blayne turned her back to her and walked farther into the house.

"Can your mother watch your children or shall I arrange

for someone to do it?" Blayne asked, then turned to face Gabriella as if nothing had happened between them.

Gabriella stared at her in disbelief. "I'm not going anywhere with you!" She walked past Blayne.

"Why are you fighting me?"

Gabriella turned around. "Are you deaf? I said I'm not going! Not going! Not going!"

Blayne stood her ground. "Go pack," Blayne said without a hint of agitation. "I have a meeting in Boston this evening, and I'll have to rush as it is."

"And here I thought you were semi-intelligent. I...am... not...going...understand?" Gabriella ground out, mocking her.

Blayne was in front of her in two strides, grabbing her by the hair as her other hand pulled her against her hard. "I have tried nicely...don't fight me, lady. I can chew you up and spit you out before you know it. Now get your ass moving. We're leaving," Blayne said between her teeth.

"Fuck you!"

Blayne kissed her hard again and tore the front of her blouse. She released Gabriella, who fell back on the sofa and stared at her in horror. "Get out of here!"

Blayne grabbed her again and began to tear the rest of her blouse off. When Gabriella tried to grab her hair, she found herself pinned underneath Blayne.

"Get ready or get fucked, understand?" Blayne hissed, her face so close to her that Gabriella saw the anger in her eyes.

"Get off me!" Gabriella said as her nerves began to shatter.

"Say no...say it...I would rather fuck you than take you back with me," Blayne said to a horrified Gabriella.

"Get off me, please." Gabriella whimpered as she tried to push Blayne away.

"Yes or no, honey. Answer now or I won't care what you say after ten more seconds like this."

"Yes, I'll go with you. Just get off me."

Blayne searched her eyes and got off her. She held her hand out to help Gabriella up. Gabriella chose to ignore it and got up on her own.

"If you're thinking of backing out of our deal, don't. You wouldn't like me when I'm angry," Blayne threatened.

Gabriella stared at her, not sure whether to believe the threat. Who could she count on to help her against someone like Blayne? The truth was there was no one. Joseph was far away. And her mother…

"I'll make sure that your mother is not pulled into this," Blayne said, almost as if she knew what Gabriella was thinking.

Gabriella took a few steps away from Blayne as she put her arms around herself to cover her nakedness. "I don't want to see him," Gabriella said as she began to cry. "He didn't want me."

Blayne stared at her back and for a brief moment felt like going to her and comforting her, but the thought quickly disappeared as she lifted her chin, effectively disconnecting herself from what she was doing.

"Call your mother. I think it would be best if the children stayed with someone they know. As to your husband…you can call him later," Blayne said coldly.

Gabriella faced her now with tears falling down her face. "No wonder my father wants to see me…" Gabriella said in disgust.

A question formed in Blayne's eyes. "Meaning?"

"If he's surrounded with the likes of you…no wonder he's looking for needles in a haystack." Gabriella meant the comment to hurt, and she took great pleasure when she saw the recognition of the insult in Blayne's eyes.

"You're quite right. None of us is what Arthur wanted," Blayne said without blinking an eye. "We've all come up short."

Within two hours, they were getting onto a private plane. They flew out of a small airport in Princeton and were scheduled to arrive in Boston in less than an hour.

Blayne looked toward Gabriella, who had not said a word to her in the last hour.

"If I feel you can't handle things with the family, I'll take you back home," Blayne said suddenly.

Gabriella searched her eyes in surprise. At that moment, Blayne saw all the fear she'd been hiding. Gabriella turned away for a second, then looked down at her hands before she spoke.

"Why does he want to see me?"

"Because he can't hide from the truth. He's out of time." Blayne looked out her window. They were taking off. She couldn't wait to get off the plane.

"I don't understand," Gabriella said, looking at Blayne's profile.

Blayne said nothing.

"Did you mean it?" Gabriella asked softly.

Blayne looked back at her now.

"What?"

"Did you mean it when you said you would take me back?" Gabriella held her breath.

Blayne looked at her for a moment without saying anything. "Yes."

Gabriella looked down at her hands again. "This is going to be unpleasant."

"Yes, it is. Chaz will probably be aggressive, and Diana will react very much like I do actually."

Gabriella looked up in fear. "Like you?"

"She's headstrong and opinionated, but no, not exactly like me, if that answers your question. I can handle them." Blayne looked Gabriella straight in the eye.

"Are they…?"

"Chaz is my brother. Diana is your sister and mine," Blayne clarified. "Chaz will resent you and Diana is antagonistic toward everyone."

Gabriella looked down at her hands again. "And your mother?"

"My mother will do as I say."

Gabriella looked up at Blayne again. "She must hate me."

"Perhaps, but she'll play along," Blayne reassured.

"Yes, I can see that people have a hard time saying no to you," Gabriella said with a touch of anger.

"They learn quickly it's best not to try."

Gabriella's gaze challenged her. "I'll take you at your word."

"I have given it to you, and I'll keep it," Blayne said with a smile that was meant to frighten her. It did.

"I believe you will. Therefore there will be no need for a repeat performance of your behavior toward me."

Blayne stared at her.

Gabriella did not look away as she waited for an answer.

"As you wish."

"I do."

Chapter Three

Blayne and Gabriella checked into the Harbor Inn in Boston. Gabriella looked around and admired the hardwood floors, the Victorian-styled furniture, and the oriental carpets that filled the inn. They were taken to a suite that faced the city rather than the atrium.

Blayne got on the phone as Gabriella went into her room.

After freshening up, Gabriella went out to the sitting room they shared and found that Blayne was still on the telephone. Gabriella walked around the room. She looked out the window, admiring the city at night. She respected preservation of the past, and the inn was a perfect example of that with its exposed brick and granite walls.

The sitting room had all the modern conveniences, such as data ports and high-speed Internet access, yet it was all hidden within the old. Patiently, Gabriella waited for Blayne to finish her call.

"No, call Armand and tell him we want to subcontract his tankers." Blayne noticed Gabriella and motioned for her to sit down. "Yes, Paul, no more than two million. Call me back on my cell. I have a dinner meeting. All right, bye."

Blayne took a good look at Gabriella, and it was obvious to both of them that she liked what she saw.

"Will you be long? What time shall I be ready to leave tonight?" Gabriella asked nervously.

"We won't be leaving tonight. I'm not sure how long my meeting will run. I've spoken to the hotel, and they'll have a car take us tomorrow morning."

"How far is it?"

"Oh…less than an hour," Blayne said.

"Why not tonight then?"

"Because I'm tired. And it'll be late. It'll be best if we arrive tomorrow morning."

"Best for who? For you?"

"No, for you!" Blayne barked out as she stood up. "Chaz and Diana are probably already waiting for you. Mother was upset when I left, but she's a loose cannon when she feels threatened. And Arthur, as much as he thinks he can handle them, he can't. I have this meeting and I'm tired. I could send you ahead, but I won't. I said I would try to…" Blayne trailed off in exasperation.

Gabriella watched her walk toward the window and stare out at the city.

The phone began to ring. Blayne closed her eyes for a moment, then opened them again and walked over to pick it up.

"Hello?"

"Blayne, I haven't heard from you. Then I picked up a message that you had checked into the Harbor Inn." Arthur sounded winded.

"Yes, we checked in about an hour ago," Blayne said as she looked toward Gabriella. "I have Gabriella here with me."

"She's there? In the hotel with you?"

"Yes, we should be arriving sometime around midmorning tomorrow." Blayne had not broken eye contact with Gabriella.

"I knew you would bring her to me. I knew you would," Arthur said. "Thank you. Thank you for doing this for me."

Blayne was silent. Arthur was obviously very emotional, and she was afraid to allow herself to feel. Arthur was dying. Her father was dying.

"I..." Blayne looked down for a moment as her eyes began to tear up. "We'll both be there in the morning."

"Thank you."

"Good night, Father."

"Good night, Blayne."

Blayne hung up the phone with her back toward Gabriella.

"You love him, don't you?" Gabriella asked in surprise.

Blayne's shoulders straightened as she turned toward Gabriella.

"Yes, I do have feelings, Mrs. Matheson. If you prick me, I do bleed," Blayne answered sarcastically.

"I didn't mean it that way," Gabriella said softly.

"How did you mean it then?"

"I just thought..." Gabriella looked down.

"You just thought that a bitch like me can't possibly feel, is that it? Well, I feel a lot of things as you obviously know...or would you like to be reminded?" Blayne asked menacingly.

Gabriella looked up. "Does he know?"

"Know what?" Blayne was not only angry, but also confused.

"About you!"

"What the fuck are you talking about?"

"He doesn't know, does he?"

Blayne suddenly understood what she meant, and her features showed the shock.

"He doesn't know then." Gabriella sounded like she had the upper hand. "What would he say if he knew how you've treated me?"

"What would he say if he knew you liked it?" Blayne

shot back.

"You attacked me!"

"Tell him and I'll tell, too."

"There's nothing for you to tell."

"Some may believe you, some may not. Will your husband believe you? Will your children believe you? Will your mother believe you? I can be very convincing." Blayne purred with enjoyment.

Gabriella stared at her in horror.

"Don't play this game with me. You'll always lose. Now go to sleep. We'll leave early in the morning. Order dinner from room service. I'll be back when I'm done with my meeting. And don't get any ideas about flying the coop, my little dove, because if you try to jump ship, I'll come after you. And believe me...you don't want that." Blayne took a step closer and Gabriella one back.

"Well, I can see you understand," Blayne said with a smile.

Blayne walked up to her and kissed her on the cheek. "Good night, little sister."

Gabriella looked up to meet her eyes and saw the hatred behind those words.

"You're not my sister," Gabriella said, trying to control her nerves.

"No, I'm not," Blayne said as she leaned closer to her. "And if I were, it wouldn't change a thing."

Gabriella looked up at her again with a shocked expression.

Blayne laughed out loud at Gabriella's reaction.

"You're disgusting," Gabriella said as she went to slap her.

Blayne held her hand and looked like she was about to strike her herself.

"Don't push, little sister. Don't push," Blayne said.

She then released Gabriella's hand and left her alone in the room.

The trip to Quincy was quiet. Blayne had been reading the paper or talking on the phone. Gabriella made no attempt to engage her in conversation.

Quincy was obviously rich in history; it boasted manicured lawns and scenic shorelines. Blayne noticed Gabriella's interest.

"There's a lot of history that took place here. Quincy is called the city of presidents. The second and sixth U.S. presidents, John Adams and his son John Quincy Adams were born here. I can arrange a tour if you like." Blayne did not wait for her to answer as she read her newspaper again.

"That might be nice. Thank you." Gabriella only saw Blayne nod, acknowledging that she had heard her, but nothing else.

The limousine then pulled into a private drive. And as the car turned around a clump of trees, the house became visible in the distance. Gabriella took in a deep breath and Blayne looked up, smiled, then looked back down to her newspaper.

The house was impressive, to say the least, with its columns and manicured hedges and colorful flowerbeds. When they pulled up, Blayne opened the door and got out without waiting for the chauffeur to come around. She then put her hand out for Gabriella to take. Gabriella looked up for only a moment, then gave her hand. As she got out of the car, the front door opened, and there next to a man dressed in a morning coat stood an elegantly dressed woman with golden hair. Her features seemed familiar and Gabriella looked toward Blayne and saw the resemblance.

"Yes, she's my mother," Blayne said, still holding her hand. "Come."

"Hello, I'm Abigail Aston-Carlyle." Abigail put her hand out to Gabriella.

Both women shook hands. "Hello, I'm Gabriella Matheson."

"Yes, my dear, I know who you are." Abigail tried to smile as she spoke.

Gabriella felt uncomfortable and looked down. Blayne was beside her and her hand was on Gabriella's back. "Let's go inside," Blayne said as she guided Gabriella away from her mother. She spoke to the majordomo as she passed him. "Henry, our bags are in the car."

They walked into the hall and Gabriella could not help but be impressed. She looked around, noticing the original paintings by Monet and Tintoretto. On one wall, she saw a Rembrandt. There were sculptures by artists she recognized that, in her opinion, should be in a museum. The walls were covered in rich creamy Muslim silk paper and the antiques were exquisite.

"Blayne..."

Blayne turned toward an older man walking toward her who only had eyes for Gabriella. Blayne made the introductions.

"This is Arthur…"

Gabriella shook his hand and could not break contact with the eyes that she'd had questions about for an eternity.

"You do have my eyes," Arthur said with a smile.

"Yes." Gabriella pulled her hand back and looked away from him.

"This doesn't please you, I see," Arthur stated the obvious.

"My eyes became an invisible wall between me and my father," Gabriella said with a touch of resentment.

Arthur looked toward Blayne. He saw no compassion there, as he expected. "Did he mistreat you?"

34

"He was my father, he loved me," Gabriella said with conviction.

Arthur stood straighter and became silent. Blayne stepped in.

"Ahh…Here's another member of the family. Come, Gabriella, let me introduce you to *our* sister Diana." Blayne took Gabriella by the arm and guided her to where Diana stood, watching as the introduction took place.

Blayne glared at her in a warning as they approached.

"Diana, this is Gabriella Matheson, our sister." Blayne added the smile as she locked eyes with a defiant Gabriella.

Gabriella nodded. "Hi."

Diana looked her over and ignored Gabriella's salutation.

"I guess it could be true. Your eyes are the same color as Father's. Although I would hardly base parentage on something as minuscule as that."

"Diana, play nice," Blayne said jokingly, but the warning was received just the same.

"I don't pretend to be anyone's daughter. I wish I wasn't here," Gabriella said defensively.

"Then why are you here?" Diana shot back. "If not for the money that my father might leave you?"

Gabriella stared at her in disbelief. "What's wrong with you people?"

"Oh, dear, we have a saint in our mists," Diana joked.

"Diana!" Blayne's voice became menacing.

"You know what, you're right. There's no need for me to be here," she said as she turned toward Blayne. "I did as you asked. I came here. Now I want to go home."

Blayne looked at Gabriella for a moment before speaking. "Diana is as upset as you." Blayne then turned to Diana as she continued to speak. "*She*, however, is acting worse than usual!"

Gabriella then directed her comment to Diana. "I don't want to take anything from you. I wish I had never been told anything at all. And I just want to go home now, please," Gabriella said the latter part to Blayne.

Blayne then turned toward her and was about to speak when she saw the tears ready to spill from Gabriella's eyes. Blayne took her by the arm and walked her out of the foyer and into the library close by.

"I'm sorry about Diana," Blayne said softly. Gabriella had her back to her.

Gabriella then turned around, and Blayne could see the tears running down her cheeks.

"Look, I just want to go home. This was a mistake all around. You promised you would take me home," she pleaded as she walked up to Blayne.

Blayne's hands went up to her arms gently; she was about to speak when the door opened and Arthur walked in.

Gabriella turned away from him and began to wipe her tears. He turned to Blayne with a concerned look on his face.

Blayne looked away.

"Gabriella…there is so much I want to say…" His voice trailed off.

Gabriella turned back to him. "I don't want to hear it! I don't want to know you! I hate you!" She was becoming hysterical.

"Gabriella!" Blayne interceded.

"No, let her, Blayne. She has a right to be upset." Arthur took a step closer.

"That's very big of you," Gabriella said mockingly.

"I'm sorry," Arthur said sadly.

"You were always between my father and me." She began to cry again. "You were always there every time he looked at me, and I saw the hurt on his face. I saw his heart break a little at a time after every comment about my eyes. And I'm supposed to be happy about this?" Gabriella openly wept as she put her arms protectively around her body. "How could I not hate you? You took my father away from me." She sobbed. "He knew." Gabriella turned, desperately seeking solace. "And he loved me anyway."

Blayne's arms surrounded her. Gabriella sobbed as Blayne held her tightly, as she looked at Arthur who sat and looked down forlorn.

"Now I've lost him forever." Gabriella wept as she buried her face in Blayne's chest.

"No, you haven't. He loved you. Not because he had to but because he wanted to," Blayne tried to console her.

Gabriella pulled away from her.

"You can't know what it was like. You didn't have people stop talking when you entered a room." Gabriella was getting angry again. "I was always the subject of speculation. And my father...I hate my eyes." Gabriella sat exhausted, then took a deep breath.

"I just want to know you," Arthur said softly.

Gabriella looked up. "Well, I don't want to know you!"

Arthur said nothing.

"I have come. Can I go now?" Gabriella asked sarcastically.

Arthur seemed confused and looked at Blayne.

"I threatened her," Blayne clarified.

"You what?" Arthur got up indignantly.

"I told you I was not the right person for this...I..." Blayne became silent.

"Blayne?" Arthur waited.

"I got the job done," Blayne said point blank.

"Blayne!"

"Isn't that all that matters? You taught me that, Father."

Both stood their ground, unwilling to back down.

Gabriella was about to say something when Abigail walked into the room and closed the door behind her.

"Is something wrong?" She looked from Blayne to Arthur.

"No, nothing." Arthur broke eye contact and Blayne seemed to take a breath of relief.

"Gabriella, my dear, I had Henry take your bags up to one of the suites in the east wing. You'll get the full sun, and the view is lovely from there. Blayne will be next to you," Abigail said with a shaky smile.

Gabriella looked down at her lap.

"I don't think…"

"That'll be perfect, Mother. That way, I'll be close by," Blayne said as she challenged Gabriella. Both women looked at each other silently for a moment.

Arthur noticed the eye contact and found it disturbing; he didn't like the idea of Blayne bullying the young woman.

"Gabriella, would you prefer a suite in another part of the estate?" Arthur waited for the response.

"Is something wrong?" Abigail looked from Blayne to Arthur.

"She'll stay in the east wing," Blayne said.

Arthur turned to her with anger evident on his face.

Gabriella stood up. "There's no need for a place for me to sleep since I won't be staying."

Blayne walked up to her and looked down into her eyes as she took her hand gently. She spoke softly so that only Gabriella could hear. "You have a father who wants to know you and a sister that might not admit it but who needs you. Stay for just a little while and give them a chance. At least give Diana a chance. God knows I haven't been able to guide her." Blayne waited patiently for her reply.

Gabriella looked down. She caught sight of her hand in Blayne's, and she almost became mesmerized by the rhythmic way Blayne's thumb was caressing her palm.

"Diana shares your blood." Gabriella looked up after Blayne made that statement. "Give that a chance. After your mother, she's all you have that's a part of you, too."

Gabriella seemed shaken, then nodded. "Only for a little while."

"Good enough," Blayne said with a smile.

"One day, you're going to outsmart yourself," Gabriella said to her seriously.

Blayne smiled a little. "You think so, little sister?"

Gabriella shook her head. "All right. but I'm only committing to a few days. Deal?"

Blayne smiled slightly. "Deal. Now let me show you to your room." Blayne guided Gabriella past Abigail and Arthur.

Arthur seemed surprised and impressed. He had just seen Blayne at her best. Not only had she managed to get Gabriella to stay, but she also had found a way of communicating with the woman who seemed to dislike her one minute and seek comfort from her the next. As usual, Blayne never ceased to amaze him.

Gabriella stopped in front of Abigail. "Thank you, I'm sure the room is lovely."

Abigail was a bit surprised at the earnest expression of the young woman in front of her.

"You're quite welcome, my dear." Abigail gave her a smile in return.

Blayne then put her hand on the middle of Gabriella's back and guided her out of the room.

"You seemed upset when I walked in."

"Blayne sometimes goes too far," Arthur said as he walked away from his wife and sat in a chair facing her.

"Blayne is too much like you," Abigail said sadly as she

sat.

"She bullied that girl to come."

"And what did you expect?"

Arthur looked up. "I didn't expect her to threaten my daughter!" He got up.

"They seem to understand each other," Abigail pointed out exactly what confused him.

"Oddly enough."

"Has it occurred to you that Blayne—that all the children—may feel threatened by Gabriella?"

"Why?"

"Arthur, for a brilliant man, you can be very dense sometimes." Abigail saw the negative reaction her words produced.

"Well, if I'm disappointed, it's their own fault!"

"I know Chaz and Diana have disappointed you. I know that Blayne in some ways has, too, by not settling down and having children. They love you, and your disappointment is obvious," Abigail said sadly.

"Meaning?"

"Meaning that coming up short is painful." Abigail's eyes filled with tears.

Arthur stared at her silently.

"Not being first choice is very painful." Tears now ran down Abigail's lovely face.

Arthur looked away. The truth was not always easy to take.

"Until recently, Blayne was the apple of your eye, and now not only is she dealing with the news of losing you, her father, but not being a first choice."

Arthur turned to her. "I love all my children," he said with conviction.

"I know you do. Just remember to let them know it," Abigail said, then walked out of the room.

Chapter Four

"Is she here?" Chaz asked as he walked into the sunroom.

"She's here," Diana said, staring out at the gardens.

"What do you think?" He sat next to her.

"What do I know?" Diana got up and stomped out of the room.

"Jesus! What's wrong with you?"

Chaz followed her. "Diana, talk to me."

"Why?" She stopped and faced him. "Why do you care all of a sudden?"

Chaz seemed confused. "Stop acting like a lunatic for once and talk to me."

Diana searched his face. "Were you ever glad I was born, Chaz?"

He blinked a few times, surprised by the question. "Yes, of course."

"I don't think I've ever thought you were," Diana said as a tear ran down her face.

Chaz seemed at a loss for words.

Diana walked away, and this time, he did not follow her.

"The view is lovely." Gabriella was looking out the window of her room.

"Yes, it is," Blayne said softly, looking at the woman

standing a few feet away.

"Have you always lived here?"

"I don't live here," Blayne clarified.

Gabriella turned to face her. "But your mother said…"

"I use the rooms in this wing when I stay here."

"Oh…"

Blayne smiled slightly. "I have a place I stay at in Boston, but home to me is my house on Cape Cod."

"But we were at a hotel in Boston." Gabriella was confused.

"I didn't think you would like the idea of staying at my place," Blayne said as she raised her eyebrows comically.

Gabriella smiled and shook her head. "Why haven't you told your family?"

"Told them what?" Blayne seemed confused now.

"About you," Gabriella said as she sat on the bed looking at Blayne.

"What about me?"

"Your lifestyle, Blayne."

Blayne's face became somber. "There's nothing to tell. What about you?" Blayne shot back.

"I have never…" Gabriella looked away nervously.

"What makes you think I have?"

"You're going to tell me I'm the first woman you kissed?" Gabriella asked with sarcasm.

"Yes, you are," Blayne said soberly.

Gabriella stared, understanding even less now.

"How about you, little sister?" Blayne asked. "Have you ever kissed a woman before me?"

"I didn't kiss you," Gabriella objected.

"Didn't you?"

"No."

Each searched the other's eyes, filled with denial. Blayne took a step forward and one of Gabriella's hands reached out for the bedpost. Blayne half smiled.

"We have a deal," Gabriella said suddenly.

Blayne froze. "I admit I liked kissing you. I liked touching you. Why can't you? We can both enjoy it."

"Because I don't have affairs. Because this type of relationship is not something I want to explore. Because I'm married. I can give you a million becauses." Gabriella got off the bed and walked toward the window again.

She didn't want to think about her reactions to Blayne's touch, so she closed her eyes and tried to stop her senses from reacting and remembering.

Gabriella felt the heat emanating from Blayne's body before she felt it pressed against her. It was no shock when Blayne's arms pulled her to her. Her head fell back almost the instant Blayne's mouth was on her neck.

"Blayne...we have a deal." Gabriella moaned. Blayne pulled her tighter to her as her mouth moved toward her ear, and Gabriella felt as if her body was on fire.

"Oh..." Gabriella moaned again as she turned around. Almost immediately, Blayne's mouth was on hers, hungrily begging for entrance. Blayne's hands pressed her harder against her. Gabriella felt her body melting into Blayne's.

There was a knock on the door and they both pulled apart, staring at each other with passion-filled eyes. The knock came again.

"Come in," Gabriella said as she straightened her clothing.

Arthur walked in and looked from Blayne to Gabriella and back to Blayne again. He noticed their apparent discomfort immediately. Blayne ran her fingers through her hair and looked everywhere but at him. And Gabriella seemed flushed and a bit nervous.

"The room...if you don't like it..." he said lamely.

"No, umm...it's beautiful." Gabriella looked around as

she replied. Her eyes looked away quickly as soon as they touched Blayne.

Arthur looked from one to the other. "Is everything all right? Has Blayne threatened you again?"

Blayne shot him a look. "Absolutely, I had the best teacher!"

"Don't go too far, Blayne," he threatened.

"Or you'll what?" she egged him on.

"She didn't do anything." Gabriella came to her defense as she took a step toward Blayne.

"When I walked in..." He paused and looked from Gabriella back to Blayne. "I'm sorry, Blayne."

"Don't apologize, Arthur. You were quite right." She walked past him and left the room.

"Blayne..." he called after her, but she didn't acknowledge him and did not turn back.

Arthur then turned to Gabriella. "I just wanted to make sure you were happy with your rooms." He was about to walk out when he was surprised by her question.

"Why didn't you ever try to see me?"

Arthur turned to face her. "I...I always thought there would be time later," he said. "I don't have a good reason, Gabriella."

She stared at him accusingly. "Did you love my mother?"

"Yes, yes, I did," he said. "I wish..." He looked away.

"You wish?"

"I wish things had been different."

"How different? Different that you hadn't seduced her and left her pregnant, or different that you had tried to be a father to me?" Gabriella was pulling no punches.

"Different that I would have stayed with her, yes, and been a father to you," Arthur said.

Gabriella was surprised at the admission.

"I'll leave you to settle in. Abigail has planned a special lunch for you. See you downstairs at one." He then left her with much to think about.

Blayne walked out to the verandah of her bedroom. She leaned against a wall and closed her eyes. *Why have things changed?* she asked herself over and over.

Blayne was angry with Arthur and with herself. And of course, he had been right to question her. She had practically assaulted Gabriella twice. She was more than angry at him for putting her in the position she found herself in, and she was angry at herself for losing control, not only of the situation, but of herself.

She had never really thought about a mate. Somehow there had always been a goal to surpass or a deal to close. Her competitive and independent spirit had always challenged her to try harder and excel yet again. She never lacked for escorts or romantic interests, but a relationship? She knew she liked women for a long time, but there had never really been one she would have taken a chance of being found out by seducing her. A mate was something she never thought about and had never needed. She was a self-contained individual. And now it seemed that her whole world had become unstable in a matter of days.

First, Arthur, her father…was dying. And second, she had been expected to bring Gabriella to him and at record speed because time was not on their side. How had he thought she could get Gabriella to come? At that moment, she resented him for putting her in that position again.

Blayne had to also admit that she not only hurt Gabriella by the cold and calculating way she had manipulated her, but she had also tried to…

"Dear God!" She ran her fingers through her hair in disgust at herself.

I practically forced myself on her in her living room. Blayne also realized no one had ever made her feel the things she felt when kissing or touching Gabriella. When she had Gabriella half-naked under her, she suddenly understood the meaning of lust. If she had remained that way a moment longer, nothing would have been able to stop her from… from?

Blayne took a deep breath and closed her eyes again. She didn't like what was happening to her. At all. She was yanked from her thoughts by a voice next to her.

"You okay?" Diana asked.

Blayne looked at her, then looked away. "Yes."

"What do you think of her?"

Blayne took a moment before answering. "She's not what I expected."

"Better or worse?"

"Different."

"You aren't going to make this easy for me, are you?" Diana was about to walk away when Blayne grabbed her by the arm.

"Wait, I'm sorry. I'm just…" She trailed off and released Diana. Blayne took a few steps toward the rail. "Give her a chance, Diana."

"A chance for what?"

Blayne turned to face her. "I've always been too busy. I'm sorry I wasn't…" She turned away again.

Diana waited. Blayne had never seemed this unsure, and that intrigued and concerned her.

"I think she's someone that if you allow her into your life she'll always be there for you," Blayne said.

"You like her, huh?"

Blayne took a few more steps and ran her fingers though her hair again. "Let's just say she's had a lot dumped on her and…what do I know?" She became angry.

"I don't understand you."

"I don't understand me, either."

"So you think I should give our sister a chance?"

"She's not my sister!" Blayne said harsher than she had intended. Blayne turned to Diana. "Talk to her. She's of your own blood. She's your sister."

"So are you, Blayne," Diana said accusingly.

Blayne looked at her. "I haven't really been good at it, have I?"

"You've sucked at it."

"She won't. Give her a chance."

Diana stared at her for a moment longer, then left her alone on the verandah.

A few minutes before one in the afternoon, Gabriella went down for lunch. As she was walking down the stairs, she was taken aback by a very attractive man looking up at her. He reached his hand out to her with a charming smile on his face as she reached the bottom of the stairs.

"Hello, I'm Chaz."

Gabriella shook his hand as she searched his face. The likeness to Blayne was uncanny.

"Sorry I didn't mean to stare," Gabriella said, returning his smile.

"It's okay I get that a lot. Blayne and I look a lot alike."

"You wish," Blayne said, coming down the staircase. "I am definitely much better looking."

"But I have the right equipment," Chaz teased, but Gabriella noticed that his smile did not reach his eyes.

"Some of us don't need it." Blayne went in for the kill. "And the ones that do don't know how to use it."

Blayne stood next to Gabriella for a moment looking at her. "Ready to go to lunch?"

"Yes." Gabriella smiled.

"Shall we?" Chaz offered her his arm.

Blayne stiffened as Gabriella took Chaz's arm.

They were served chilled lobster salad on plates made to look like seashells. Gabriella looked around the table and noticed how comfortable they all were with the wealth that surrounded them.

The lobster salad was delicious, and the perfectly chilled white wine was divine. Gabriella noticed that the only person who hadn't tried to engage her in conversation was Blayne, who seemed to be brooding at the other end of the table.

"So you have two kids?" Diana asked.

"Yes…"

"Where is their father?"

"Joseph, my husband, is in Chicago on business."

She looked toward Blayne, who looked away with a frown.

"You're an artist." Chaz smiled charmingly.

"I'm a sculptor."

"Are you any good?" Diana asked tactlessly.

"Well…"

"You're being modest, Gabriella," Arthur said proudly, then he turned to the others. "She has several pieces on display at galleries in New York City."

Gabriella looked back at him. He looked at her and smiled as he said, "She's very talented."

"I bet she is," Chaz said crudely, then smiled innocently.

"Chaz!" Blayne finally spoke up. Chaz hadn't fooled her for a minute.

"What?"

"Enough, you two," Arthur intervened.

Abigail took the opportunity to jump in. "We have a lot of interesting things to see here in Quincy, Gabriella. Have you visited Massachusetts before?"

"Yes, once."

"Oh, really?" Abigail smiled.

"Yes, I came to visit Harvard."

"You tried to attend?"

"I got accepted," Gabriella said and looked down.

"You didn't go?" Diana asked with renewed curiosity.

"No, my scholarship fell through." Gabriella could not hide the disappointment even after all the years that had passed. She still remembered how proud her mother and father had been. She also remembered the day she found out that the money she needed to attend would not be available.

Arthur stopped eating as he noticed the disappointment that showed on his daughter's face.

"Blayne went to Harvard," Diana broke the silence.

Gabriella looked up and met Blayne's eyes, which looked back at her softly now.

"She also attended Harvard Law," Diana added. "She was even the president of the Law Review."

"Blayne has never known when to stop," Chaz said in jest.

"At least she finished, Chaz!" Diana blurted.

"Look who's talking," he said with a smirk.

"Children!" Abigail reprimanded them.

"Blayne, are you staying for a few days?" Arthur redirected the conversation.

"Blayne not work?" Chaz teased.

"Blayne? Will you stay?" Diana looked toward her older sister expectantly.

"Leave her alone. Blayne is busy," Abigail cut in.

"Gabriella, how about I show you the sights around Quincy?" Chaz offered.

Gabriella was about to speak when Blayne cut in. "Gabriella and I already have plans for today, Chaz," she said, then turned toward Diana. "And yes, Diana, I am planning on staying." She then turned to Gabriella. "Are you ready, Gabriella?"

Gabriella blinked and nodded. "Yes."

"Let's go then. Mother, lunch was fantastic as always," Blayne said as she got up from the table.

"Yes, thank you so much for lunch. It was wonderful," Gabriella said as she got up confused and a little angry at Blayne's behavior.

Arthur knew what Blayne had done. Gabriella was obviously going along with it, but it was not right that Blayne should bully her around. He had to have a talk with Blayne. Perhaps Abigail was right; it certainly would explain Blayne's volatility of late.

"Have a good time, you two. We'll expect you for dinner." Arthur turned toward Blayne. "We dine as usual at eight in the evening."

"I remember, Father," she said, challenging him.

"Run along then and have a good time."

Blayne walked around the table and out of the room with her hand possessively on the middle of Gabriella's back.

Almost as soon as they walked out of the dining room Gabriella showed her displeasure. She was headed toward the staircase when Blayne grabbed her by the arm and turned her around.

"Where do you think you're going?"

"We've got to get one thing straight here. You are not my ruler. I'm not going to let you keep bullying me around, understand?" Gabriella put her hands on her hips and she was fuming.

Blayne seemed unfazed. "Where are you going?"

"I'm going to get my purse from upstairs."

"You won't need it. Come on, let's go." Blayne grabbed

her by the arm again and stopped as Gabriella yanked her arm away.

"No."

Blayne was about to grab her again but stopped when she heard the door open and Arthur walked toward them.

"I thought you two were going sightseeing."

"I just have to get my purse," Gabriella said defiantly.

"Okay, hurry, go get it." Blayne knew when to pull back.

Arthur smiled as Gabriella went up the staircase. He turned in time to see Blayne looking at her, as well.

"I would like to talk to you when you two come back."

Blayne turned to face him. "All right."

"Where will you take her?" Arthur was trying to make some peace between him and Blayne. He didn't like the estrangement that seemed to be developing.

"Adams National Historic site, Quincy Armory, Bethany Church, United First Parish Church, and the Adams Crypt. After that, we'll just see what she might like to see next. I would also like to show her the museum if possible."

"The itinerary sounds perfect." Arthur kept trying to make conversation with his daughter. "Did you fix things with Armand?"

"Yes, he was able to get the tankers for under two million."

"How did Betancourt ever agree to that?"

"I'm having dinner with him next week," she said matter-of-factly.

Arthur stared at her sternly.

"It was part of the package," she said without batting an eye.

Arthur looked furious. "Is that how you conduct business with my company?"

"What the hell are you talking about?"

"I never wanted a deal so much that I would condone what you have done or plan to do," Arthur said in disgust.

Blayne's face paled.

Gabriella was at the top of the staircase and had heard Arthur's last comment.

Blayne's face became as cold as marble.

"Who are you to talk to me about morals?" Blayne's voice was low but as cold as steel. "How do you think I got her here if not by threats and intimidation? That's what you taught me."

Arthur was livid.

"I'm your creation. I'm just like you. Just as moral and as much of a lecher…"

Arthur slapped his daughter so hard it made her stumble back. Gabriella cringed at the sound. He stared in horror at what he'd done. Blood was oozing out of Blayne's lips. She stared back at him with all the anger that his accusation had produced in her.

"I don't sell myself. My reputation in the business world is unquestionable. Personally, however, I'm proving to be unscrupulous. I know you don't like what you see in me right now. Perhaps, it's something in you that you're hating." Blayne saw what she had just said register in his face. "But don't feel bad, Father, by the time I'm your age, I might surpass even you," Blayne finished venomously.

Arthur was taken by surprise by what she said.

"I'm sorry I shouldn't have said those things to you. Your behavior has always been—"

Blayne cut him off. "No, it hasn't. I've done just about everything to win, except sell myself. As for personal relationships…I'm a complete failure just like you. I won't get married just to please you. I won't live a lie, not even for you. And unlike you, when I find the person who makes me *feel*, I won't run away." Blayne was seething.

"What's gotten into you? You're out of control." Arthur stared back at her.

"Perhaps unlike you, my behavior is making me sick." Blayne meant the retort to sting. "So don't feel bad, *Daddy*," Blayne said sarcastically as she wiped the blood from her mouth with the back of her hand. "I deserved the slap. I have truly been your daughter these last few days," Blayne said with such coldness that Arthur took a step back.

Gabriella came out of the hold that kept her unmoving. She walked down the staircase, and Blayne looked toward her and their eyes locked. It caught Gabriella by surprise to see the wounded look in them.

Gabriella passed by Arthur and walked up to Blayne who looked at her without saying a word. Gabriella reached into her bag and took out a handkerchief. She gently wiped the blood from Blayne's lips all the while looking deeply into her eyes. Blayne then took her hand and held it as she bowed her head.

Gabriella caressed the bruise that was already appearing on the beautiful face. "Come on…we'll get you an ice cream cone. Any flavor you want," Gabriella said tenderly.

Blayne was surprised, and a smile slowly appeared on her face. "Any flavor?"

Gabriella nodded. "Any flavor." She then took her by the hand and led the way.

Arthur stood rooted to the spot. Again he was speechless and confused by the interplay between Blayne and Gabriella.

If I didn't know any better… He didn't allow the thought to continue.

Gabriella had, in her silence and indifference, let him know what she thought of him. With Blayne, however, she had shown incredible tenderness. The lamb led the wolf and the wolf, Blayne, had docilely followed. Arthur didn't like what was going through his mind at the moment. He didn't like it one bit.

Blayne and Gabriella walked side by side to the garage. Blayne opened a side door and stepped in. Gabriella's mouth dropped open at the row of cars lined up in front of her. They passed a black Rolls Royce, a red Jaguar XK8 convertible and a powder blue Porsche. Blayne then stopped in front of a car Gabriella was not sure she recognized.

"This one is mine. I keep it here." She opened the passenger door and Gabriella sat down. She looked around and admired the lacquered wood and the softness of the kid leather. The dashboard was filled with clocks and buttons… she was sure the car could fly. The vehicle exuded strength and power. And she inwardly told herself that it suited its owner.

Blayne got in the driver's seat and smiled at her. "You like it?"

"It's an amazing looking car. What is it exactly?"

"It's a Bentley Arnage T. The most powerful car in its history," she said excitedly.

"I can see you really like it. Somehow I didn't think you were the sports car type."

Blayne turned to her with a confused expression. "What do you mean?"

"This car…it looks…maybe it is you. It's conservative on the outside, then it surprises you with the unexpected on the inside."

Blayne smiled. "I'm the unexpected, huh?"

"I've never known anyone like you, Blayne," Gabriella said sarcastically.

"If I analyze that, I think it might be a compliment." Blayne then turned the key, and as the engine roared to life, the garage doors automatically opened.

Chapter Five

Blayne and Gabriella had been on the road for a few minutes when Gabriella noticed the seriousness of Blayne's face. The woman was obviously deep in thought.

"This hasn't been easy for you, either, has it?" Gabriella asked.

Blayne looked at her, then back to the road, looking straight ahead. She seemed to be debating whether to answer.

"I wish I had never met you," Blayne said suddenly, still looking straight ahead.

Gabriella looked down at her hands and said nothing.

The silence began to cut at Blayne. She could not resist the desire to look toward Gabriella, and as she did, she saw the tear roll down her face as Gabriella turned to look out the window.

Blayne then pulled over to the shoulder, turned off the engine, and faced Gabriella.

"That didn't come out right," Blayne said apologetically.

"I know what you meant," Gabriella said, still looking away.

"I'm sorry," Blayne said as she placed her hand over Gabriella's.

Gabriella then looked at her, and Blayne could now see the tear-stained face.

"Are you?" Gabriella asked softly.

"Yes," Blayne said as she looked down at their hands. "I don't like hurting things. I don't want to hurt you. I want…" Blayne stopped talking, looked up at Gabriella, then just as quickly looked down again.

"What do you want?"

Blayne looked up again, and this time, she didn't turn away when she spoke.

"I want you like I've never wanted anything in my whole life," Blayne said passionately. "I want things I don't understand and yet I know…I want you so much, Gabriella, that I'm drowning in this," Blayne finished desperately.

Gabriella pulled her hand away.

Blayne's whole semblance changed and her body stiffened at Gabriella's withdrawal. Without saying another word, Blayne started the car and pulled back into traffic.

"Didn't work, huh?" Blayne joked after a few minutes of silence.

Gabriella turned toward her with an incredulous look on her face.

"Hey, be a good sport. I like you. I want to…Well, you know what I want. When I'm like this, I'll say anything. No harm no foul, okay?" Blayne kept smiling. "Oh! There's something for you to see." She pointed to a building across from them. "That's the Quincy Museum."

Gabriella looked at the museum and followed Blayne's lead. Anything was better than the silence that had occurred between them a moment before.

"Let's stop there first," Blayne said, then maneuvered the car in that direction and drove into the parking lot.

"And, Blayne," Gabriella said as she looked at her again.

Blayne put the car in park and turned toward her, as well.

"No more games, okay?"

"Okay, no more declarations of love," Blayne said with a smile. "But I won't promise not to try to get you to bed," she said cheekily.

Gabriella could not believe her gall. She then got out of the car.

Blayne's gaze suddenly showed incredible sadness. She took a deep breath, then got out of the car with a smile. It was as if a cloak had been put back in place to cover what lay beneath. She would never allow her feelings to surface again.

The day passed pleasantly enough. They visited many of the historic places that the small town of Quincy, Massachusetts, had to offer. Blayne was attentive and politely distant. Gabriella could not find any fault in her behavior, yet she didn't quite understand why Blayne's politeness seemed to bother her.

They had drinks together in a place near the ocean. They spoke of Gabriella's interest in art and her upcoming exhibition. Blayne asked her many questions, yet managed to keep all the subjects safe ones.

"What are your children's names?" Blayne asked.

"Elena and Christopher," Gabriella said with a smile. "Elle is thirteen and Christopher is eleven."

"Elle?"

"Her nickname. I call her Elle."

"I don't know why I thought they were younger. How long have you been married?"

Gabriella looked at her for a moment, then answered. "Sixteen years."

"That's a long time being married to someone you don't love," Blayne said, looking down at the cup of coffee in front of her.

"Why do you assume that I don't love my husband?"

Blayne said nothing for a moment as she searched Gabriella's eyes.

"Have you talked to him lately?"

"Two nights ago," Gabriella said defensively.

"Does he know you're here?"

"No, I'm calling him tonight to explain things to him."

"I see."

"You see what?"

"You receive news that has shaken up your entire life, and you haven't told him. He doesn't even know you're here. And you would never have kissed me back if you loved him. Affairs are not your style." Blayne waited for the response, knowing by the look on Gabriella's face that she had struck a nerve.

The silence again grew between them. Gabriella was the first to break eye contact.

"We should start back," Blayne said suddenly. "We have to get ready for dinner and Arthur wants to talk to me. Unless you want to order dessert or something."

"No, I'm ready. Let's go," Gabriella said as she began to rise.

Blayne paid the bill, and they drove back to the house in silence.

"Hello?"

"Hello, Mama, how are Elle and Chris?" Gabriella asked.

"They just finished dinner. There's a message from Joseph leaving a number where you can reach him tonight. You haven't told him, have you?" Elena knew but asked anyway.

"No, I haven't. I will when I call him later tonight."

"Have you…?"

"Yes, I've seen him," Gabriella said right away.

There was silence for a moment.

"Are you all right, Leila?" Elena asked with concern.

"I...I'm really confused, Mama. One minute, he seems very attentive, then he will do something utterly horrendous."

"Has he upset you?" Elena's voice showed her anger.

"No, he's been very kind to me. Blayne, however, has been..."

"Blayne?"

"They have issues. They all have issues. I met the rest of the family. What a gruesome group." Gabriella expressed all her frustration.

"And Arthur?"

Gabriella noticed the concern in her mother's question, and it surprised her somehow.

"What about him?" she asked testily.

"How is he...with the cancer and..."

Gabriella said nothing for a moment. It could not be possible that her mother still cared for this man, she told herself. The idea of that angered her. What about her father? Had she loved Arthur even after marrying her father?

"He doesn't seem sick to me. If this is a trick, so help me...I wouldn't put it past them..." Gabriella trailed off.

"Leila, do what your heart tells you. But remember you might not get the chance later. Really think about this."

"I will, Mama, I will."

Gabriella then spoke with each of her children before taking a shower and getting ready for dinner.

Blayne knocked on the door to the library and waited. She went in after hearing Arthur tell her to come in.

"Why the knocking? You always just walk in," Arthur said from behind his desk.

"I figure if we observe the rules, things will be handled

better," Blayne said bluntly.

Arthur said nothing for a moment, then got up and walked around his desk. He pointed for her to sit. She sat and crossed her legs. He sat down, too.

"Blayne, I know these last few days have been difficult."

"Yes."

"Your mother has pointed out to me that I have not handled things very well. And I must admit, I agree. I should never have…" Arthur was progressively becoming more uncomfortable. "I should never have hit you. I'm sorry."

Blayne remained silent.

"At least you didn't bruise."

Blayne smiled a little and looked down. She'd spent a good thirty minutes applying makeup to cover up her bruised cheek.

"No, no bruise," she finally said.

"Good."

Arthur then got up and started walking about the room. "Did you and Gabriella have a good afternoon sightseeing?"

"Yes."

"How long will you be staying?"

"For as long as she decides to."

Arthur stopped pacing and looked at his daughter for a moment in confusion. "Why is that exactly?"

"Because I promised to take her home if she needed protecting."

"From who?" Arthur asked indignantly.

"From you. From all of you." Blayne stood and faced him.

"I see, so you're her protector. And who protects her from you?"

Blayne's face became dark and menacing. "No one can

protect her from me, not even you."

Arthur looked at his daughter as if for the first time.

"You don't forgive me for this indiscretion, do you?"

"Indiscretion? Is that what she is?"

Arthur stared at Blayne with speculation.

"If I didn't know any better, I'd say you're in—" He stopped himself.

Blayne saw the thought written on his face and she paled. Suddenly, they both found themselves with empty space between them.

Arthur looked at her, not believing and not daring to utter a word.

Blayne sat back down, and he continued looking at her profile.

"I want to hear you say it," Arthur said.

"Is there a need?"

"Yes, I think there is." He waited, hoping beyond hope that the words would never leave her lips.

"There's nothing to tell. The lady is not interested," Blayne said coldly. She couldn't see his face but could almost feel the shock register in him.

All she had to do was deny it, but the words had just come out. Blayne got up and walked to the window and looked out. "She doesn't want me," she said softly, not caring how her comment would be received.

Arthur looked at his daughter in horror. He just stared at her as a million things entered his mind. This must be the reason the subject of her private life was not open to speculation, he told himself. And if Blayne had to want women and not men, why Gabriella? Why his daughter?

The impact of those two questions hit him hard. He sat down because he thought his legs would give out. He noticed she had not moved from where she stood. Blayne's face mirrored a sadness he had once known and now feared.

He didn't understand this choice, but he couldn't help but notice the pain he saw in his daughter's face. He loved her and something inside him hurt to see her this way. She was his daughter, too. But this could not be. He could not and would not allow it to go any further.

"Blayne, have you?"

Blayne turned to face him, and it surprised him to see the unshed tears in her eyes.

"You must let this go."

She looked down as she played with her fingers, then turned around to look out the window again.

"Consider it done," he heard her say softly.

Blayne did not participate in any of the conversations during dinner. If asked a direct question, she made her answers concise. Arthur kept looking at Blayne, expecting her to shake off her detachment and was disappointed when it never occurred.

"Blayne, how about a game of chess?" Diana suggested. Blayne continued to play with her uneaten dessert, seemingly oblivious. "Blayne!"

"What?" Blayne looked up testily.

Everyone turned toward her.

"I asked if you wanted to play chess after dinner," Diana repeated.

"No, I have papers to go over," Blayne said as she got up. "Please excuse me. Mother, dinner was splendid as always."

"You hardly ate, my dear. Are you feeling all right?"

"Yes, fine," she said as she left the room without so much as a look toward Gabriella.

Gabriella, on the other hand, kept looking in Blayne's direction all throughout dinner. She was disappointed to see that Blayne had not even looked in her direction when leaving.

Arthur turned and noticed the sullen look in Gabriella's face. "Shall we all have our coffee in the Chinese parlor?"

"Yes, of course, Arthur, if you like." Abigail smiled.

"Shall we then?" Arthur stood and the rest followed.

The conversation was general enough so the possibility of discord was eliminated. Gabriella realized that Blayne's presence was something she had taken for granted. Blayne's absence made Diana reach out to Gabriella.

"When is your exhibition scheduled for?" Diana asked as she sat next to Gabriella.

"In the spring. We're looking at mid-April right now."

"How many pieces will be on display?"

"Between fifteen and twenty."

"Why the uncertainty?" Diana seemed genuinely interested, which pleased Gabriella.

"Well, I have ten completed, and I'm working on two more right now. I'm borrowing three to just show. It kind of depends on inspiration." Gabriella smiled at Diana.

"Hmm…" Diana nodded and smiled back. "I'd like to go if you don't mind."

Gabriella was surprised but pleased. "Yes, I'd like that. I'll make sure you get an invite."

"Lovely."

"Yes, do send it, my dear. I'm sure we would all like to try to attend." Abigail nodded.

"Yes," Arthur added. He then noticed Gabriella's pensive expression. "Is that all right with you?"

"I'll have to think about it. I don't want my mother to be upset." Gabriella directed her comment at Arthur.

"I understand, your mother will be there." Arthur looked down at his coffee cup.

"My mother has always been there," Gabriella said, and Arthur's head shot up, meeting her gaze.

She was accusing him, he realized, and he had no defense. The room had become uncomfortable for all of them.

"The lady that fragile?" Chaz asked sarcastically.

"Chaz!" Arthur reprimanded.

"Well, it does take two, you know."

"We can always count on your crassness, Chaz," Diana said in disgust, looking at her mother.

"Well, it's true! She didn't get made by only one of them. Her mother is responsible, too!" Chaz blurted out with his usual thoughtlessness.

Abigail closed her eyes and looked away.

Gabriella stood up. "You're quite right, Chaz, it does take two. But my mother didn't abandon me. She faced it. And yes, she lied. She lied to a lot of people, but she did what she had to do to keep me."

"Yes, of course that excuses her." Chaz had sunk his teeth in and was not about to let go.

"Chaz, be quiet!" Arthur stood, as well.

Abigail covered her face with one hand as her elbow leaned on the arm of the chair she sat in.

"No, it doesn't excuse her lying to me. It doesn't excuse her lying to my father." Tears fell down Gabriella's face. "She went against everything that she is and she believes in for me. She loved me enough to do anything it took to keep me."

"Chaz, don't be such an ass," Diana said.

"Please, Chaz," Abigail implored her son.

Arthur was fuming but said nothing. Chaz sat down and said nothing else. The room was silent for a moment.

"If you'll all excuse me," Gabriella said as she left the room.

"Chaz, you can be a real asshole!" Diana spat out.

Abigail got up and left the room, too. Arthur looked censoriously at Chaz and Diana, then left after Abigail.

Chapter Six

Blayne looked up at the knock on the door.

"Come in."

She was surprised to see Gabriella. Blayne stood as she noticed the tears on her face.

"I want to leave now."

"What happened?"

"You promised to be there and you weren't. I don't want to know them. I just want to go home. You can't stop me! Please, Blayne, take me home."

Blayne walked around the desk and toward Gabriella.

"If you aren't taking me, then I'll leave on my own!"

"Gabriella, wait." Blayne grabbed her arm.

"Let go!" She tried pulling out of Blayne's grip, but Blayne held on tighter.

"Calm down. What happened?" Blayne pulled her closer.

"I just want to leave." Gabriella sobbed.

Blayne pulled her into her arms. Gabriella tried pulling away, then her arms went around Blayne and held her tightly as she cried.

"You weren't there," Gabriella said as she cried.

"I'm sorry," Blayne said as she kissed her hair, holding her tighter. "It's all right now. I won't leave you alone again."

Blayne kissed her head and her face gently. Gabriella

turned her face and she looked up. Blayne's lips kissed her softly. "I'm sorry. You won't be alone again. I promise." She caressed Gabriella's face.

"Blayne, please…"

"Shh…" She kissed Gabriella again, then pulled her deeper into her embrace.

Arthur walked in unannounced. They both turned to him still holding on to each other. Gabriella released Blayne and took a step back. Arthur stared from Gabriella to Blayne.

"Blayne, I need to speak to Gabriella alone. Then I would like to speak with you." Arthur left no room for argument. Blayne felt like a schoolgirl being caught in an infraction, being sent away to be punished appropriately later. She looked toward Gabriella, then back to Arthur.

"No."

"No?"

"No."

Arthur was visibly angry. "I want to speak to Gabriella, leave us, Blayne!"

"No."

"Very well. Will you concede to speak with me then?" Arthur could barely control his anger. She had disobeyed him, and he was angry. He had told her to stay away from Gabriella.

Blayne felt Gabriella's hand in her own. She looked down, then up to Gabriella's face, and what she saw surprised her.

"Blayne?" Arthur said impatiently.

"It's all right. Go on. We'll talk again later, I promise," Blayne said gently with a reassuring smile to Gabriella. With that one action, Gabriella had sealed Blayne's fate. There was no retreat now. She was in for better or for worse.

Gabriella then left them alone. Arthur said nothing for a moment.

"What was that I walked into?" He voiced his anger.

"You walked into what you created. What happened? What did you all do?" Blayne lashed back.

"Chaz, as usual, was himself."

"Why didn't you control the situation?" Blayne asked accusingly.

Arthur just stared at her.

"What?" She walked away from him. "What do you expect from me?"

"I want you to stay away from my daughter!"

Blayne felt the blow even if no physical contact had been made. She stood silently, waiting and searching his eyes for the man she knew.

Arthur broke eye contact and walked toward a chair and sat down.

"I'm not responsible for what you all do. I can't stop her from coming to me, Arthur." Blayne ran her fingers through her hair as she spoke. "I hate this."

Blayne turned away and Arthur now looked to her.

"Have you always been this way?" he asked out of nowhere.

"You mean have I always liked women?"

"Yes, that," he said uncomfortably.

"I've never given it much thought."

"If you've never given it much thought, then why her? Why now?" He stood up in agitation. "I'm dying, Blayne. Why now?"

"Why Elena Agramonte? Why her when you knew you shouldn't?" Blayne asked, then looked away sadly. "I don't know why. It just is."

"Then walk away," Arthur insisted as he stood up.

"Like you?" Blayne stood, as well.

"All right! Yes, like me!"

"I can't." Blayne lost all her anger as she said the words.

"I can't."

"I want you to go then."

Blayne looked at him and allowed her eyes to show the hurt in them.

"It's best, Blayne."

"Is it that easy for you to turn me away?"

Arthur looked away. "It's best."

"For you."

Arthur looked her in the eyes unmoved. "Yes, for me."

"No."

"No? What is it with you and no?"

"I promised her I would be here until she left. I won't break that promise. I won't." Blayne stood her ground.

"You also promised me something."

"What do you want from me, Arthur? I love her, goddamn it!" Blayne covered her face as the magnitude of the words that had come out of her mouth hit her.

"You just met her! This is sick, Blayne!"

Blayne remained silent, then she looked up and just stared at him. "Is that how you see me, Father? Am I something repugnant to you now? How am I different? Don't you think if I could tear this out of me I would?" Blayne waited for answers that she knew would never come. "I don't know how to stop it."

Arthur looked away from her and walked around the chair he had been sitting in.

Blayne breathed in deeply.

I love her. Oh, God, I love her, she thought over and over as she looked around the room in desperation.

"Perhaps it's a chemical imbalance or something."

She looked at him, not believing what she had just heard. "A chemical imbalance?"

"Yes, a psychiatrist might be able to help you," he said hopefully.

Blayne looked down, then turned away from him as she walked toward the window. It was still light out. Nothing had changed, yet everything in her world had.

"I have no chemical imbalance. I don't think they've invented a cure for loving someone. You should know that," she said sadly.

"It's not right for you to take advantage of Gabriella."

She turned around and faced him. "What?"

"Don't manipulate her. She has a life. Diana needs her. She has a husband."

"She doesn't love him!"

"Does she love you?"

Blayne remained silent. He had his mark and went in for the kill. "What about her children and her mother? Elena is old-fashioned. Would her children understand? Even if you were to seduce Gabriella...would she be able to walk away from her husband and children to be with you?"

Blayne met his eyes as hers filled with tears. "I love her." The truth of her words hurt. Those words she never thought she would utter cut at her.

"If you love her, then let her go."

The tears ran freely down Blayne's face. Arthur had never seen her like this and her weakness touched his heart. "It'll be for the best," he said softly. At that moment, Arthur knew he had convinced her.

She nodded as the tears continued to fall. Blayne looked down, then up and met her father's eyes again.

Arthur looked away quickly. "All right then. In time, you'll see that you did the right thing."

He looked at Blayne again before he left her in the library and again his chest tightened in pain. Blayne would keep her word, he knew that. Arthur also realized that they would never be close again.

"Hello, Joseph."

"Gabriella? Where are you?"

"In Massachusetts."

"What's going on?" He didn't hide the anger in his voice.

"I had some rather upsetting news less than a week ago," she said, yet she realized it seemed like ages. So much had happened in such a short period.

"How could you just take off and not tell me?"

"I'm sorry. I guess I wasn't thinking."

"Yes, thinking is not your forte, is it?"

"No, I guess not." Gabriella felt drained.

"I'll be home Thursday. We finished up earlier than expected. Remember we're dining with the Metcalfs on Saturday. Will you be back by then?" He sounded like he was in a hurry.

"Um…yes, I should be." Gabriella was feeling the strain of the day.

"Good, I'll see you no later than Saturday then."

Before she could speak, he hung up, and it occurred to her that this is the way they spoke. Neither of them really cared for the other anymore. They acted out of habit, of what was expected rather than the need to connect. The usual feeling of restlessness began to overtake her. At these times, she went to her studio. Gabriella thought about trying to find Blayne. Instead, she opted for a walk. She needed to be active.

Gabriella walked around the grounds. Even though it was dark, the flora was still visible and the fragrance was wonderful. She leaned down to admire a flower when she heard footsteps. Gabriella turned and saw Arthur approaching. She stood up straight, almost bracing herself in finding herself alone with him.

"Those are Chinese lilies." He pointed to the flowers that she had been admiring moments before.

Gabriella looked at them again, then away.

"I'm sorry about everything." Arthur waited expectantly for her next move.

Gabriella looked at him and said nothing. Almost by an inner understanding, they began to walk side by side.

"You have a lovely family," he said.

Gabriella said nothing as they continued to walk.

"I would like to meet my grandchildren, Gabriella," he said. "I'm not asking for forgiveness. I know only time, perhaps, could gain me that with you. Unfortunately, time is the one thing I don't have. I won't say anything to them. I would just like to see them once before I die. Please grant me that." Arthur's words sounded sincere and made her nod her agreement.

"Thank you," he said, moved by her generosity.

"I think I'll go in now," she said.

"I've spoken with Blayne."

Gabriella turned toward him. "And?"

"She won't be bossing you around anymore."

"I can take care of myself. I don't need you fighting my battles for me," Gabriella said irately.

"Blayne sometimes…is too aggressive."

"At least she knows what she wants and she fights for it."

"Is that an attribute you admire?" Arthur eyed his daughter curiously. He had not expected Gabriella to be defending Blayne or excusing her.

"Yes."

"Is that how you see yourself?"

"No, I'm not like her," Gabriella said sadly. "I wish I was."

"Gabriella?"

"It's been a long day. Good night." She walked away from him.

"Good night," Arthur said as he watched her walk back into the house.

Blayne walked up to Gabriella's door and was about to knock when she seemed to change her mind. She took a step back, and as she was about to walk away, a voice pulled her back.

"Not up for it, huh?"

Blayne turned to see Gabriella approaching her with a slight smile.

"Scared of me?" Gabriella teased.

"Yes," Blayne smiled back. "You are too formidable of an adversary," she played along.

"I see."

"What do you see?"

"I have power." Gabriella was thoroughly enjoying the game.

"Is that what you think?" Blayne laughed.

"That's what I know." Gabriella stood in front of her now.

Blayne couldn't have looked away if she wanted to. Her eyes were fused with those of the lady in front of her. She was about to reach out for Gabriella when something in Blayne's eyes changed. Gabriella felt the withdrawal before Blayne had taken a step back away from her or seen it clearly in her eyes.

"I concede the field. You win." Blayne waved her hand flamboyantly, but they both knew that Blayne had in effect backed down out of fear.

Gabriella decided to change the subject. "You were looking for me?"

Blayne was forced once more to look into her eyes. "Yes."

She stood without uttering a word searching Gabriella's face.

"I spoke with Arthur out in the garden."

Blayne blinked and snapped out of the trance she was in. "Are you all right?"

"Oddly enough, yes." She looked down. "He asked if he could see the children before…" She trailed off, then looked up to see the pain of it register in Blayne's eyes.

"You said yes," Blayne said sadly.

"Yes, I did. You must think I'm crazy," Gabriella said as a nervous giggle escaped her.

"No, I think…" She looked away.

"You think?"

Blayne looked at her again. "I think you're very generous."

Gabriella kept looking at her expecting words that never came. Blayne was not fighting her. Blayne was pulling away. She could feel it.

"Are you all right?" Gabriella was the one who asked this time.

"Of course, why shouldn't I be?" Blayne laughed and took a few more steps away from Gabriella.

"I feel…"

"You feel?" Blayne asked seriously.

"I can't explain it." Gabriella began to fidget.

"Don't worry. I won't leave you alone. I'll be with you 'til I take you home," Blayne said, not able to look away from the gaze that begged her for answers of questions that had not been asked.

"Did Arthur say something to you?" Gabriella probed.

"Arthur and I talked, and we agreed on things." Blayne looked away.

"You two made decisions about me?" Gabriella's face showed her anger.

"Gabriella, it's late. We can talk in the morning." Blayne was about to walk away when Gabriella took a hold of her arm.

Blayne looked at the hand that hung on to her, then back at Gabriella's face. "Tomorrow. We can talk tomorrow."

"No, I want to talk now," Gabriella insisted as she opened her bedroom door.

"No," Blayne barely whispered as Gabriella pulled her into her bedroom.

Gabriella closed the door behind them, then turned to face Blayne. Blayne took a step back and put some distance between them.

"What did you want to discuss?" Blayne said, unable to hide what she felt.

"What's wrong?" Gabriella asked as she got closer.

"Nothing." Blayne took another step back and turned to look out the window beside her.

"It's dark. You can't see anything out there now."

"I have good eyes," Blayne said with a nervous laugh.

Gabriella stared, not believing what she was seeing. Blayne was incredibly nervous, and all she seemed to want to do was to run. Run away from what?

Blayne couldn't stand the silence and in exasperation she turned to finish the conversation and just leave. "You wanted to talk."

Gabriella stood in front of her now. There was no escape. "You're shaking."

"Am I?" Blayne's response was barely audible. Her gaze was locked with the woman in front of her.

Gabriella's hand caressed her bruised cheek. Blayne closed her eyes and leaned into the touch. "Does your face still hurt?"

Blayne's eyes opened slightly. "Not now."

"Blayne" was all that Gabriella said before her lips

kissed the bruise on the cheek.

Blayne's hands had a life of their own. They went to take a hold of Gabriella, then pulled back.

"Is that better?" Gabriella said huskily.

Blayne could hardly breathe as her senses were filled with all that was Gabriella. She closed her eyes tightly and opened them again with a look of desperation.

Gabriella leaned in closer and kissed Blayne's cheek closer to her mouth this time. "Is that better?"

Blayne was speechless. She was giddy and confused. Her senses were on overdrive, yet she felt powerless to push Gabriella away from her. Her entire body was alive and throbbing with a need to connect that she had never experienced before. She could feel her body pulling her, tugging at her to just give in and end the misery of the overwhelming hunger that consumed her. "Gabriella," she groaned, and her breath came in short gasps.

Gabriella went to take a step back when Blayne's hands pulled her hard against her. Her mouth was on Gabriella's neck before she realized what she was doing. Blayne's hands traveled over the body she longed to possess.

"Blayne, no, wait." Gabriella tried pushing her away.

Blayne could no more stop than rid herself of the pounding in her ears. She had become raw nerves and yearning flesh as her body was filled with the pangs of an unquenchable desire to touch and feel and taste the woman in her arms. She ripped Gabriella's blouse, and her mouth found a nipple to suck.

"Ah…" Gabriella grabbed Blayne's hair and tried pulling her off. "Stop!"

Blayne left the breast and grabbed her by the hair and kissed her hard. She could taste blood in her mouth and she liked it.

"No!" Gabriella pushed her hard.

Blayne stood in front of her dazed and confused. She stared at Gabriella's mouth now stained in blood and her eyes widened in horror. She saw the fear on Gabriella's face, and she took a step back.

An overpowering sense of panic overtook her and she had a hard time breathing. One hand reached for her chest as the other reached for the wall. The room was beginning to spin and all she could do was try to breathe, but no air seemed to reach her lungs.

"Blayne?" Gabriella was above her. Fear showed in her eyes as Gabriella took her in her arms and held her tightly as they slid to the floor. "It's all right, breathe. Breathe. Relax and breathe."

Blayne began to breathe easier, never for one moment losing eye contact with Gabriella.

Gabriella could still see the hint of panic in those eyes. She held Blayne closer and caressed her, offering soothing words of reassurance that all was well. What was it about this woman that touched her so, Gabriella asked herself. One minute, Blayne was as fragile as a child and the next she was mauling her. And now her eyes mirrored such fragility that they tugged at something deep inside her.

"It's all right," Gabriella said as she caressed her hair and kissed her forehead. She heard a whimper from Blayne, and as her eyes met the woman's in her arms, she saw the fear reappear. "You frightened me."

"I…" She began to breathe deeply again. "Help me up and let me get out of here." Blayne tried getting up but found that her legs did not listen. Tears filled her eyes. "My body betrays me." She cried in exasperation.

"Blayne…"

"Help me up! I have to go." Blayne tried again and Gabriella helped her to her feet.

"Blayne…"

Blayne did not look her in the eye again.

"I'm sorry. I'm sorry." Blayne let go of Gabriella as she tried to walk away.

"Are you all right?"

She turned to look at Gabriella again.

"No, I'm not. I have to go. I'm sorry. I can't do this. I want you. Is that what you want to hear? I want you!" Blayne's tears fell over her cheeks again. "I'm not strong enough. I can't do this. Something is wrong with me." Blayne wept as she tried wiping the tears away with the back of her hand.

She stared at Gabriella who still stood inches away from her.

"Release me from my promise," Blayne said.

"You frightened me" was Gabriella's reply.

"Release me," Blayne begged, almost in a whisper. It was more of a prayer. Blayne was asking for so much more.

Gabriellà looked at her and realized that the words in the car earlier had been real. The knowledge of that touched her more than she cared to admit. Blayne was overwhelmed with such emotions that were now visible.

"I can't," Gabriella said, barely able to believe what she had just said. "I'm afraid."

Blayne was barely able to contain the sob that escaped her. Gabriella walked up to her and put her arms around her and leaned her head against her neck. "I'm afraid."

Blayne's arms went up and held her to her and breathed in the scent of her hair. "I need you."

Gabriella looked up, and this time, Blayne's lips felt soft and warm. Gabriella pulled Blayne closer. Slowly, their hands traveled over each other's bodies. The caresses were soft and gentle. One by one, garments were removed, and once they were both naked, Blayne pulled back and looked over the body of the woman she was unable to resist. When her gaze went back to Gabriella's eyes, she knew she would never be able to let her go.

Their mouths met just as their bodies fused together. Their need grew and touches became bolder. Somehow they were on the bed. Blayne felt Gabriella's body moving beneath her as her head went back and she felt the first wave of pleasure overtake her.

Then almost as if time had lapsed in ecstasy, Gabriella was above her and both became one. There was no question or doubt; they gave into the need to satisfy something that was stronger than both of them. Neither knew how it happened, but almost as if something inside them still felt the fear hiding, waiting, they held on tightly to each other, and that is how they fell asleep and how the first rays of the morning found them. Both still in each other's arms, both bodies still clinging with a need to connect.

A dull and distant pounding woke Gabriella from a sound sleep.

She opened her eyes and realized that someone was knocking on the door. Gabriella then turned her head and came upon Blayne's eyes. She looked down and saw their interwoven limbs, and the events of the previous night filled her mind.

"Gabriella?" The knocking persisted. "It's me, Diana."

Gabriella looked in horror at Blayne. Blayne put her finger on Gabriella's lips and whispered. "Tell her that you just got out of the shower and you're dressing and that you'll meet her downstairs in a bit."

Gabriella nodded and did as Blayne suggested.

"Okay, I'll see you downstairs then," Diana said as her footsteps faded away.

Blayne turned to look at Gabriella as she was still staring at the door.

"Good morning," Blayne said with smile as she tightened

her hold around Gabriella's midriff.

Gabriella then turned toward Blayne and tried pulling away. "What's wrong?" Blayne sat up next to her.

Gabriella still did not look at her.

"Don't worry, darling. Diana will understand," Blayne said as she leaned down and tried to kiss her. Gabriella pushed her away and sat up as she slid her legs over the bed.

"I don't intend to tell her," Gabriella said bluntly. Gabriella turned toward Blayne after the silence was not broken.

They stared at each other, and Blayne realized that something was wrong. "Explain quickly before I get the wrong idea," Blayne said anxiously.

Gabriella got up, grabbed a robe, and put it on. She was unable to look at the woman who just a moment earlier had been in her arms. Looking at Blayne lying naked in the bed they had shared suddenly disturbed her.

"I don't know what you expect," Gabriella said, looking away from Blayne's accusatory eyes.

"Don't do this, Gabriella."

"I'm sorry, but I don't know what you expected." Gabriella did not dare to look at Blayne.

Blayne got up and walked over to her.

"Get dressed." Gabriella turned away from her. Blayne froze at the coldness of the rejection.

Blayne was unable to move for a moment. Then with all the dignity she could muster, she picked up her clothes and got dressed. Gabriella never looked in her direction.

"You are your father's daughter after all. Welcome to the family, little sister," Blayne said as she closed the door behind her.

Gabriella shut her eyes and wrapped her arms around her body as she dropped to the ground and wept.

Blayne slammed the door to her bedroom, took a few steps, and started tearing off her clothes in a rage, then just as suddenly, she began to sob, holding herself tightly. Her whole body shook as the sobbing racked her body.

Chapter Seven

Blayne felt arms around her and tried pulling away, only to give in to the need to be held.

Diana held her tightly. Never in her life did she imagine finding Blayne so vulnerable and distraught. Her big sister was nothing if not strong and in control all the time. She had come upstairs looking for Gabriella but found she was not in her room. When she passed Blayne's door, she stopped when she thought she heard crying.

Diana walked into a scene she would never have imagined or would ever forget. Blayne was crouched in a fetal position, half-naked on the floor.

"What happened?" Diana asked as she held her sister tightly. "It's okay. You're going to be okay."

Blayne only cried harder.

An hour later, Gabriella went downstairs looking for Diana.

"Hello."

Gabriella turned around and came face to face with Chaz

"Looking for me?" Chaz asked with his best smile.

"Umm, no, but I'm glad to see you," Gabriella said amicably. "Have you seen Diana? She wanted to talk to me, and I said I'd meet her down here."

"She was here earlier. I think she went upstairs to talk to Blayne."

Chaz noticed that Gabriella seemed nervous for a moment, then she just smiled and walked toward the library. He watched as she entered it and the wheels in his head began to turn.

Something is going on here, and I'm going to find out what it is. If she thinks she can come in here and take a piece of money that should go to us, she has another thing coming.

Chaz went looking for his mother. She would help him. Surely, she didn't want to see Arthur's bastard take anything away from her children.

Arthur looked up as soon as Gabriella walked into the library.

"Oh, I'm sorry. I just wanted to get a book."

"No, no, my dear, come on in." He gestured for her to get whatever she wanted. "I'm glad you decided to stay. Please, talk to me awhile."

Gabriella sat close by. "You said I could ask you questions."

"Yes, of course." He sat and waited.

"Why now? I mean, I know that you're sick, but why?"

"When you're dying, you can't lie to yourself anymore," Arthur said.

"Lie to yourself? I don't understand."

"When there are no tomorrows, your life has to be looked at...I guess I finally looked at myself. Of all of them, Blayne was the hardest on me." He smiled and looked away. "She doesn't let me get away with what I did, not even now. And she's right. That's the difference between her and me." Arthur remained silent for a moment before looking at Gabriella.

"And what is it that Blayne doesn't cut you any slack

on?"

"Honor."

"Honor?"

"I've been very much aware of that lately. I was a cad where your mother was concerned," Arthur said frankly.

"A cad? Is that what you think you were?" Gabriella got up and turned her back to him. "You promised undying love and you got her pregnant, then left her. You were a cad? That's the least of what you were." Gabriella turned to face him as she finished her accusation.

He looked down in shame. "You sound like Blayne."

"What?" Gabriella was thrown for a moment.

"Nothing. You're quite right. I didn't think of her or you at all." Arthur looked at her without blinking.

"How could you hurt her? Even now…she wanted to know if…" Gabriella sat down, visibly upset. "My mother is the kindest, most loving woman I know."

Arthur sat again. Elena still thought of him. He closed his eyes and leaned his head back.

"Does she hate me?"

Gabriella looked up and stared at him.

He looked up into his daughter's eyes. "Does she? Does she hate me?"

"My mother doesn't hate anyone." Gabriella saw the pain register in Arthur's eyes before he got up and walked toward the window. "How could you hurt her?"

"I did love her…I want you to know that. She was the loveliest thing I had ever seen. I…wish things might have been different, Gabriella. I'm sorry," he said with regret. "You will never know how sorry I am."

"Perhaps I'm not the only one you should apologize to."

Arthur turned to face his daughter. "Would she see me?"

"Well, you do have a weapon, don't you?" Gabriella said sarcastically.

Arthur stood there perplexed.

"Send Blayne." She walked out of the library to let him think about what she had just said. Before she walked out, she could tell the last jab had hit home and hurt him.

She was angry. She told herself she had the right to be. All that he had given her up to now was heartache. And she was not about to cut him any slack because he was dying.

Gabriella closed the library door behind her, and it hit her. Her father...her father was dying. Did it matter? Yes, it did. She was more confused than before and more troubled. When she looked up, she saw Blayne, whose eyes were filled with anger and accusation.

Gabriella was frozen to the spot by the coldness she saw in Blayne's eyes. And just as suddenly, Blayne turned away from her. She walked to the breakfast room without acknowledging her presence. Diana had been walking closely behind her and stopped for a moment when she saw the exchange.

Diana watched as Blayne walked into the breakfast room, then she walked over to Gabriella. "Everything okay?"

Gabriella looked down at her hands, then up at Diana. "Yes, thank you."

"Are you and Blayne fighting again?"

"No, I don't know...Blayne is..." Gabriella trailed off.

"She's really okay. She just seems a little off-kilter. Besides the news about Father...she's...I think something is going on with her. So don't be too mad at her. She really is all right. Blayne is Blayne. I think we get angry at her because she is just so right all the time...but when I'm in trouble, she's the one I call."

"I guess I just looked to myself. I never had anyone to..." Gabriella trailed off.

"Well, you do now, don't you?" Diana smiled and slid her arm around Gabriella as she pulled her toward the breakfast room. "You have at least one sister."

Gabriella looked at Diana and smiled tenderly. "Yes, I have a sister."

For the next two days, Blayne and Gabriella stayed well away from each other, and their estrangement did not go unnoticed. Chaz in particular seemed happiest of all, not missing any opportunity to be with Gabriella.

Gabriella mentioned over breakfast that she would be leaving early the next morning, which inwardly made Blayne breathe easier than she had in the previous two days.

"Must you go so soon?" Diana asked with obvious disappointment.

"Yes, I've been away from home too long. But you'll come and visit soon, I hope," Gabriella finished with a smile as her hand covered Diana's.

"Yes, I want to meet my niece and nephew," Diana said excitedly.

Gabriella turned toward Arthur. "I'll speak to my children…then I'll call you."

Arthur smiled and nodded.

"Well, I hope I'm invited to see you soon, as well," Chaz said with his most charming voice.

"Of course, Chaz," Gabriella said cordially.

Abigail did not fail to notice, as Arthur did, that Blayne was the only one who had seemed oblivious to their conversation.

"Someday I would like to meet them, as well, my dear," Abigail said genuinely.

"Yes, I would like that, too," Gabriella said honestly. For the last two days, Abigail had been so kind to her. It hadn't been what she said so much as how she said it, and the honesty of her emotions seemed to come through.

"Does that mean you'll be leaving us, as well, Blayne?" Diana asked as she turned her attention to her older sister.

"Yes, I've been away from the office for too long. If you all will excuse me, I have some phone calls to make." Blayne got up and walked out of the room.

Blayne had called her office, advising them that she would most likely be in the next day. She went over some correspondence over the phone with her personal assistant, and when the knocking on the door broke her concentration, the irritation showed in her voice.

"Come in!"

Gabriella walked in and closed the door behind her.

Blayne met her eyes for a moment before continuing to speak to her assistant on the phone. "Matt, can you hold a moment?" She covered the receiver and directed her comment to Gabriella, who was still standing by the door. "What do you want?" Blayne did not bother to hide her dissatisfaction at being interrupted.

"I wanted…I need to talk to you before…"

Blayne uncovered the phone. "Matt, I'll call you back." She hung up the phone and faced Gabriella from the power position behind her desk.

"I…" Gabriella found it hard to speak.

"I don't have all day. Is there something I can do for you?"

"Yes, you can come here and stop making this harder than it is for me," Gabriella said as she began to shake.

Blayne only waited a moment before she got up and walked to the woman standing nervously a few feet from her. She'd told herself over and over that Gabriella would not have the chance to disrupt her psyche again, yet here she was doing exactly as she had been asked—walking toward her. Walking to what?

Blayne stood mere inches from Gabriella, still fighting to keep some distance. Suddenly, she could see the tears in Gabriella's eyes, and when Gabriella walked into her arms, she only resisted for a moment, then her arms came up and held tightly to her. A moment later, Blayne pushed Gabriella away, still trying to find reason in the insanity she knew this was.

"No..." Blayne said more to herself than to Gabriella.

It was futile to fight her body, Blayne told herself, as she tried desperately to. As Gabriella's tears silently rolled down her face, her mouth came up, and when she moaned, "Blayne..." there was no resistance left in Blayne. Blayne's mouth came down quickly and took the invitation offered, and she was not sure whose moan she heard next—Gabriella's or her own.

There was another knock on the door, and Blayne pulled away almost as the door opened. Diana walked in and found them looking away from each other. Blayne walked back to her desk and Gabriella began to wipe her face.

"You weren't fighting again, were you?" Diana asked them both in exasperation.

Blayne still had her back to her as she leaned on the desk in front of her. "Diana, please not now," she said shakily. Diana looked in her direction, noticing the unsteadiness of Blayne's response. "Diana, I need a moment to speak to Gabriella," Blayne said, trying to catch her breath. "Please leave us for a few minutes."

Diana looked at Gabriella. It was obvious that something was wrong. Gabriella had indeed been crying since she could still notice the moisture in her eyes and the way her hands shook. "Gabriella, are you all right?"

"For God's sake!" Blayne turned around now, filled with anger. "She's fine. Diana, please, just give us a moment, all right!"

"I'm not going anywhere until I know that you two aren't fighting again. So don't try and be a bully. It won't work with me, big sister," Diana said as she put her hands on her hips.

"Diana, we aren't fighting. Please, I need to speak to Blayne," Gabriella said.

"What is it with you two?" Diana asked in exasperation. "Why can't you two get along...Gabriella, why are you crying?"

"Diana! Please leave us for a few minutes." Blayne turned and faced her.

"Blayne, I am...."

"Diana, please, it's all right," Gabriella said reassuringly.

Diana looked from one to the other.

"Diana!" Blayne was losing her patience.

"Okay, okay."

Diana walked out, leaving the door open.

"Close the damn door!" Blayne yelled.

The door closed immediately. Then Blayne gave Gabriella her full attention, but now there was palpable distance between them.

Gabriella was the one who walked to her and held Blayne to her. "Don't be angry anymore, please," she pleaded.

"Gabriella, this is a mistake..."

Gabriella then kissed her, knowing that this physical connection if nothing else was the one thing that neither of them could fight. And Blayne responded, as she knew she would.

Blayne's hands caressed her body as her mouth traveled down her throat. "Gabriella...Oh, God, Gabriella."

The phone rang as someone knocked again.

"Damn!" Blayne growled. As the door was opening, she

reached for the phone.

This time, it was not Diana but Arthur who walked in. Gabriella turned away as Blayne spoke into the receiver. "Matt? I said I would…" She stopped to listen.

Arthur walked up to Gabriella who did not seem to want to meet his eyes. He was experienced enough to know that there was something going on between them. Of that he was sure.

"Gabriella dear, I need to speak to Blayne alone."

Blayne met Gabriella's eyes as she still listened to the telephone call. "Matt, schedule a meeting with them for next week and call the London office. I want them in this, too. I'll call you back within the hour. Good job." She hung up. "Arthur, Gabriella and I are in the middle of something."

"Your husband called. He needs to speak to you about your dinner party scheduled for tomorrow," Arthur said to Gabriella, but the hardest blow of the statement was visible in Blayne's face, as he knew it would be. Blayne turned her back to them as Gabriella walked out of the room without saying a word.

Blayne closed her eyes tightly. *I am such a fool,* she told herself. *She has a husband…whom she runs to. And I am standing here like a…*

"Blayne." Arthur waited for her to turn and face him. When she didn't turn around, he said her name again. "Blayne!"

"What?" she said irritably as she turned around.

"Stay away from her."

"I didn't…she's the one that…she's married, as you said," Blayne repeated as she walked around the desk and sat down. "I need to call the office. Is there anything else you wanted to discuss?"

"I…No, except that I wanted to see if you might want to go out on the boat with me this Sunday." They had always gone out on the boat at least once whenever she visited. Their love of sailing was something they had shared, and he hoped even under these uncomfortable circumstances, they would again.

"No, I have to be in LA on Tuesday, and I have to get everything ready for a meeting that we're scheduling with London," she said as she picked up the phone.

"All right. Perhaps soon then." Arthur walked out, leaving her to her work. He had lost her and he knew it. How had he managed to lose control of everything?

"Arthur? Is everything all right?" Abigail asked him as he walked out of the library.

"Yes, yes, it is, my dear."

Two hours later, Blayne walked out into the gardens from the library. She needed to find something to hold on to. Why had she lost control of herself?

Blayne Samantha Anberville had always been her own self-sufficient world. She had loved people but never really needed them. And now someone had appeared out of nowhere and in a matter of hours, that had changed. Because if she was honest with herself, Blayne had to admit that she had been under Gabriella's control after that first moment they had breathed the same air. And that realization more than anything else in her life made her tremble. Her world was dependent on another human being, and she didn't want it to be.

Blayne walked in silence, thinking and regretting every step she had taken since she had met Gabriella Matheson.

She became aware of voices and walked tentatively toward them. Blayne came upon Chaz and Gabriella sitting on a nearby bench. She couldn't exactly hear what was being said, but when she saw Gabriella quickly rise and Chaz grab her by the arm and pull her toward him, nothing else seemed to matter. Blayne felt an unfamiliar heat fill her body and an anger that took over her senses.

Why should I do anything? she asked herself. That worked until she realized that Gabriella was not welcoming Chaz's attentions. When Gabriella pushed him away and he refused to release her, Blayne's resolve disappeared and her feet could not get her there fast enough.

Chaz felt the impact before he actually saw Blayne coming. He landed hard on his back as Blayne grabbed Gabriella and pulled her to her so that she would not fall, as well.

"Are you all right?" Blayne asked as she looked deeply into her eyes. "Did he hurt you?"

Before Gabriella could answer, Chaz blurted out the inevitable. "Oh, so that's how it is, isn't it? Now it's quite obvious," he said as he got up, dusting the dirt from his clothes.

"Shut up, Chaz!" Blayne threatened.

"Or you'll what? Throw me down again? I don't think so. This time, you're the one that's going to hit the ground after I take you out, you sick fucking dyke!"

Blayne was about to strike him when Gabriella's hold on her tightened. "Don't let him goad you. Leave it be, please! Leave it be."

"Hiding behind your dyke friend?" he taunted.

Gabriella could not hold her as Blayne threw her whole self into Chaz. They both landed on the ground. She managed to hit him in the face before he threw her off. Blayne landed hard on her back, and for a moment, the wind seemed to be knocked out of her.

"Chaz! No!" Gabriella screamed.

Chaz was above Blayne and about to hit her when his fist stopped in midair as he heard the anger in Arthur's voice behind him.

"Don't you dare strike her!" Arthur yelled.

Chaz turned, and Blayne hit him hard on the chest. "You son of a bitch!"

Arthur pulled her off Chaz, and Gabriella went over to her and held her back.

"Enough!" Gabriella said to Blayne.

"Chaz, go inside. I'll talk to you later." Arthur left no room for argument.

Chaz looked toward Blayne. "Sick bitch!"

"Chaz! Go!" Arthur insisted.

As Arthur watched Chaz walk away, Gabriella directed her attention to Blayne.

"Are you all right? Did he hurt you?" She caressed Blayne's face.

Blayne pulled away from her. She hated herself for what she had just done. She had brawled like an animal over a woman! She ran her fingers through her hair as she walked to the bench and sat down.

"Blayne?" Gabriella sat next to her and tried touching her again. Blayne moved away slightly.

"Leave me alone," Blayne said as she closed her eyes and tried to disappear.

"Did he hurt you?" Gabriella asked again softly.

"No," Blayne finally answered as her eyes opened and turned to the woman sitting next to her. They just looked at each other as Arthur watched the scene unfold.

Gabriella's hand again went out, and this time, Blayne did not stop her. Her eyes closed as Gabriella caressed her face.

Blayne got up and looked down at the woman sitting on the bench. "I have to go…"

"I'll walk her back." Arthur finally spoke.

Blayne looked in his direction as if suddenly remembering he was there. She looked down at Gabriella again. She was about to say something, then seemed to think better of it.

Blayne walked away without looking back.

Gabriella watched her as she saw the distance once again growing between them.

"What happened?" Arthur brought her back to the present.

"Chaz…he tried to bestow affections that I didn't want. Blayne must have seen him from somewhere and stopped him. They…I thought he was going to really hurt her." Gabriella looked away.

"I'll deal with Chaz, don't you worry. Are you all right?" Arthur took a few steps closer to her.

"Yes…No, I…everything seems to be…" Gabriella trailed off.

"You've had a lot of shocks lately. It's understandable. And Blayne's behavior of late hasn't helped."

"Why do you automatically assume that she's to blame for everything?" Gabriella sounded angry.

Arthur surprised her by saying, "Because she is too much like me."

"But she's not you."

"You're right, of course. Maybe I don't want her to make the same mistakes."

"She said you two had talked about me. What about?" This was the perfect opportunity to find out what had been discussed.

"I told her to stay away from you. Blayne…Blayne is confused right now," Arthur said vaguely.

"Confused?"

"Yes. She's experiencing feelings she shouldn't."

"What feelings?"

"To do with you." Arthur seemed embarrassed.

"Anger is understandable."

"It's not anger."

"Then what?"

"Inappropriate feelings."

"She told you this?" Gabriella stood up.

"It wasn't exactly like that."

"What was it then?"

"Gabriella, I don't think…"

"You started this. What did she say to you?" Gabriella was really angry now. She felt betrayed by Blayne and furious at the audacity of the man in front of her for interfering and making decisions about her life.

"Gabriella, this is not something I think…"

"You started this. You seem to think you have a right to interfere in my life. You have obviously done so. I don't need you to run interference for me. I'm used to looking after myself." Gabriella was furious.

"Blayne had no right to push herself on you. She clearly told me that you did not welcome her advances. She can be very insistent." Arthur tried to explain.

"How dare you assume that I can't defend myself? I have news for you, I've been defending myself without you my whole life. It's too late now. Now I don't need you."

"I just wanted to protect you…"

"What makes you think I want protecting?" Arthur's gaze came up to meet his daughter's. Clearly, he had misread the signs. Gabriella was not a victim; rather it would seem she was an active participant. He had been wrong about this, as well.

He had assumed that Blayne had been the aggressor, and to some extent, maybe she had been, but now looking at his daughter, it was all too clear. Gabriella was the strong one here. She was more his daughter than even she knew. And Blayne… Blayne would be the one who would be hurt.

"I think it's time I went home," Gabriella said as she walked away, leaving Arthur alone in the garden with yet another realization.

Arthur sat on the bench. He seemed quite old as he sat there; an incredible sadness showed on his face. Now he knew exactly what would happen.

Gabriella left that night. The cab pulled up to the house and her bags were placed in the trunk. She walked up to the door that the cab driver was holding open for her, then stopped before getting in. She turned and locked gazes for a moment before she turned and entered the cab.

Arthur had stood by the front door and turned to see Blayne standing by the window that Gabriella had looked toward before getting into the cab. She had not bothered to look at Arthur to say goodbye.

Chapter Eight

"Vivian?" Gabriella opened the door wider to allow her cousin to come in.

"Hi," Vivian said as she passed Gabriella.

"Did we have plans for today?" Gabriella closed the door and followed her cousin into the living room.

"No," she said as she sat down.

Gabriella sat on the other end of the same sofa.

"Well, it's nice to see you, Viv."

"How did it go? And why didn't you tell me?" Vivian waited for an answer. "And when were you going to tell me? You've been back over forty-eight hours."

"How?"

"Tia Elena was beside herself."

Gabriella ran her fingers through her hair.

"I had a lot of…there have been…I'm so confused," Gabriella finally said.

"She told me all about it, Gabriella…I'm sorry. I think Mom is still in shock."

Gabriella nodded.

"How was he?" Vivian asked as she put her legs under herself, facing Gabriella on the sofa.

"I don't know…you can't know anything about someone in a few…" Gabriella didn't finish the sentence. Blayne suddenly filled her thoughts. She got up and walked toward a window. "I mean…you can't make life-changing decisions…" She ran her fingers through her hair in exasperation.

Gabriella turned toward her cousin, her face showing all the fears and uncertainties she was feeling within. "Oh, Viv, I met someone."

Vivian blinked twice in surprise, then got up from the sofa. "You what? Wait! Wait! You mean…?"

Gabriella began to pace around the room nervously. "Oh, what a mess. I never thought…I mean I…" Her control began to slip.

"Holy shit," Vivian said in a trance. Vivian then noticed her usually composed cousin fidgeting nervously. "Gabriella?"

Gabriella turned toward her. Vivian was surprised to see the tear-filled eyes looking so miserable and lost. She walked to her cousin and put her arms around her. "Oh, Christ, you're scaring me," Vivian said as she held her tighter.

After a while, they both sat down. Gabriella avoided looking at Vivian.

Vivian placed her hands over Gabriella's. "Talk to me. You and I have always confided in each other. Remember when I cut math in high school and Mom found out?"

Gabriella looked up with a smile as tears rolled down her face. Vivian tightened her hands around her cousin's, encouraging her to talk.

"Oh, sweetie, it's going to be okay, tell me," Vivian coaxed.

Gabriella got up. "No, it won't. Nothing will ever be okay."

Vivian tried another approach. "Well, we can't always control our feelings. Why don't you tell me about it?"

"I can't…" Gabriella put her arms protectively around herself.

"You're not the only woman to have an affair. It happens,"

Vivian insisted. "It's not something that women plan on."

Gabriella remained silent.

"Look, if it's that important…Jesus! Divorce your husband. I think he's an asshole anyway."

Gabriella still remained silent.

"This is more than an affair, isn't it?" Vivian asked cautiously.

Gabriella looked up at her and again tears ran down her face.

"Oh, Gabriella." Vivian realized this was serious. Something was really wrong.

"I couldn't stop it, Vivian. It was stronger than I was." Gabriella covered her mouth to control the sob. "Oh, my God, what am I going to do?"

Vivian got up and tried to console her cousin again. "Then maybe this is a good thing."

"No!" Gabriella became agitated and took a few steps away from her.

"Is it one-sided?"

Gabriella shook her head.

"Then you can make it work. A divorce won't be easy, but…"

"I can't."

"Why not? If you want him so much and he wants you."

"It's not that simple," Gabriella murmured barely above a whisper.

"I know it's not, honey. The kids would understand. They're great kids."

"Oh, God." Gabriella covered her mouth.

"Is he married?" Vivian dreaded asking.

"No."

"Does he want a relationship with you?" Vivian couldn't understand, so she kept fishing for answers.

Gabriella nodded. "I wanted just to stay in those arms for the rest of my life." She closed her eyes as tears escaped them. "I've never wanted anyone like..." Gabriella said miserably.

"If he wants you, too, then why not?"

"There is no he, Vivian!" Gabriella turned and looked her straight in the eyes.

"I don't understand. You said..."

"Blayne is Arthur's stepdaughter..."

"I don't understand..." Vivian was confused. Then Gabriella could tell that her words had finally sunk in.

Gabriella sat down.

Vivian sat opposite her. The news had caught her off-guard, and she remained silent.

Gabriella looked toward her, then down again.

Vivian shook her head. "You say she feels the same?"

Gabriella nodded, still looking down.

"You said you had an affair...you mean you...?" Vivian trailed off not knowing exactly how to pose the question.

Gabriella got up and walked toward the window again. She stood looking out.

Where are you, Blayne? Gabriella closed her eyes and leaned her head back before saying, "Yes, I slept with her."

"Get out of my sight!" Arthur yelled at the top of his lungs.

"Father..." Chaz appealed to Arthur's sense of familial responsibility.

"I'm only your father when it's convenient to you." Arthur put some distance between him and Chaz in exasperation.

"I admit I acted badly. How many times can I say I'm sorry?"

Arthur faced him in disbelief. "Bad judgment?"

"Yes, bad judgment. I admit it."

"Chaz, you accosted my daughter and you were about to strike Blayne, your sister, when I showed up! That's more than bad judgment." Arthur paced the room. "It's time that you grew up."

"Father…"

Arthur turned to face him. "I won't be around to pull you out of things anymore." Arthur felt and looked tired.

"I can help Blayne in the company."

Arthur looked at Chaz, and the surprise of what he just heard was evident in his face.

"I know that I have to take charge of my life. I've done nothing else but think about what a disappointment I've been to you all night. I want to try."

Arthur knew this was probably some kind of ruse on Chaz's part, but he was also hopeful that his son actually meant what he had just said.

Arthur walked toward a chair by the fireplace and sat in contemplation.

Chaz stood next to him. "I won't disappoint you this time."

"All right. I'll talk to Blayne," Arthur finally said.

Chaz smiled. "You won't regret it. I promise."

"All right, my boy. All right." Arthur sounded tired. He let his head fall back on the chair as Chaz left the room.

"Blayne?"

"Make it fast, Diana, I'm on my way out," Blayne said impatiently into the telephone.

"I didn't even know you were leaving."

"I'm sorry…I should have told you. I had some business come up that I had to take care of immediately. As a matter of fact, I'm on my way to the airport."

"Where are you going?" Diana kept the conversation going.

"London," Blayne said as she was going through some papers on her desk.

"I can meet you there," Diana said hopefully.

"What?" Blayne looked up.

"Well, I thought I might meet you there. There's so much I want to talk to you about. You're the only one I can talk to about this."

"Is something wrong?" Blayne sounded rushed.

"No, I mean…well, I can't talk to Daddy or Mother. And Chaz…well, you know how Chaz is."

"What is it?" Blayne looked at her watch. She was running late, yet she felt guilty about just hanging up on Diana.

"It's Gabriella…"

"Oh, God…can we…I mean…I'm running late, Diana. What about Gabriella?" Blayne sounded more sarcastic than she had meant to.

"Hey, I thought you two had made up."

"We…we aren't fighting. It's…what about Gabriella?" Blayne ran her fingers through her hair.

How can I do this? I can't do this! Blayne's resolve seemed to be vanishing. "I can't do this right now. Please, give me a little space right now, okay?"

Diana could hear the frailty in Blayne's voice, and she didn't understand it. Again she was filled with feelings of dread. "Blayne? Are you okay?"

Blayne closed her eyes.

"You can always talk to me, you know. You don't have to be the strong one all the time."

Blayne's eyes remained closed. "I can't…"

"Okay."

"Diana…it's not that…" Blayne trailed off.

"When you're ready."

"Thanks."

"So? London then?" Diana asked hopefully.

"Yes." Blayne smiled. "Yes, London."

Gabriella found the discussion with her cousin draining. Vivian had obviously been surprised. They agreed to meet again the next day. It was almost a relief to both of them when Vivian had remembered she had planned on having lunch with a friend.

Gabriella went to her studio and uncovered the piece she had begun working on before leaving. She wet the clay and began to mold it. She never noticed the time; her mind was focused on the piece in front of her. Her every touch was an extension of a part of her, and it took her by surprise when her mind caught up with what her hands had begun what seemed like a lifetime ago. The clay had come to life and as she stared at it, she felt the inevitable pull.

"Who is she?" a male voice said from behind her.

Gabriella gasped and turned around. "God, you scared me," she said to Joseph as she breathed in deeply.

"Sorry. Who is she?"

Gabriella turned to face the image that even now called out to her. "No one you know…" She covered the figure with the cloth next to it and turned to face him again. "Why are you home so early?" She looked toward the clock on the wall.

"I thought you and I should talk," he said, pulling a chair over.

"Talk?"

"Well, you were away for a week. You haven't been yourself since you got back. I want to know what's going on."

"I can't. The kids…" Gabriella said, getting up.

"I called your mother. She'll pick them up for you. I told her I'd pick them up later." He was firm.

"You always take care of everything." Gabriella could not keep the resentment from her voice.

"I like to have things spelled out, yes. The dinner party was a disaster. It was as if you weren't even there. What's going on with you?"

She walked over to a counter and washed her hands under the sink.

"I went to Massachusetts to meet my father." She turned around and sat a few feet away from him. "It's complicated."

"Obviously. I think you should explain, don't you?"

She got up and paced, stopping abruptly. Gabriella turned and looked toward her husband. Her eyes searched his, looking for something. And then she looked away sadly.

Why couldn't it be you? she thought, shutting her eyes.

"I'm the daughter of Arthur Aston-Carlyle." she said and looked at him yet again.

Say something and comfort me...Take me in your arms and tell me it's going to be okay, she thought and waited. *Take me in your arms and make me love you. Make me forget.*

"You're kidding," Joseph said in disbelief. "The shipping magnate Arthur Aston-Carlyle?"

Gabriella nodded.

"Wow," he said as he got up and walked past her.

Gabriella closed her eyes as he did.

Blayne! her soul screamed.

Blayne hung up the phone after speaking with Diana and sat behind her desk.

Gabriella... she thought as she leaned her head back and closed her eyes. *Traitor! How could you leave me like this? Damn you!*

Blayne felt an incredible pain in her chest and breathed deeply. She could almost hear Gabriella calling her name.

"I don't want this. I don't want this!" She got up quickly, picked up her briefcase, and walked out of her office.

"I don't understand. How? I mean..."

"My mother knew him in Cuba," Gabriella said as she looked down. She felt tired and didn't really want to go into all the details now, but she knew there was really no choice. Joseph would not let up until he knew everything.

"Why didn't you tell me?"

"It all happened so fast. You were away. I...I'm still not sure about anything..." She trailed off.

"Are you his daughter or not?"

"Jesus! Leave me alone!" Gabriella began pacing. "I'm so confused right now. I don't know whether I'm coming or going. Stop! Just stop, okay?"

"Gabriella, calm down," he said as he came closer to her. "Let's take this one step at a time."

"Why don't you listen?" Joseph seemed confused, and she continued. "Why can't you know what I need? Why don't you see me?" Tears rolled down her face.

He was completely taken aback by her emotional outburst. "I...I don't understand. Of course I understand you. Look, we don't have to talk about his right now if you don't want to."

He walked up to her and she went into his arms with a desperation that frightened her. She buried her face into his chest and searched for that oneness she so desperately needed.

"Hold me, Joseph...please hold me. I'm so lost. Please... hold me." His arms went around her and held her closer. Her face went up to him and her lips sought his mouth. Her mouth met his hungrily and opened, offering him her passion. When his lips failed to give her what she so desperately wanted, she pushed him away.

"What the hell is wrong now?" He tried reaching for her, and she cried harder. "What's going on?"

"Leave me alone, please. Just leave me alone." She turned her back to him.

"We can't go on like this," he threatened. "You come on to me, then you push me away. We hardly ever have sex anymore. I still want you," he said uncharacteristically.

"I'm sorry."

"I'll go pick up the children at your mother's. Shall I pick up some dinner?" The conversation turned as it always did into the normalcy of denial.

She nodded quietly.

He walked out of the studio and left her holding herself. Suddenly, all her desire and shame became pain, and she doubled over and fell to the floor.

"Blayne...Blayne..." she cried.

Chapter Nine

Blayne sat and let her head fall back on the seat. The flight to London would give her the distance she desperately sought. Her eyes closed, and as they did, she held back a word she longed to say.

She sat up and looked out the window and saw the distance growing, and she could no longer stop from whispering the one word that her heart could not stop saying over and over again. "Gabriella." She said it softly, reverently, and she allowed herself to savor it.

She turned on the music in her headphones, trying to change her thoughts, but was caught prisoner by the melody playing. Instead of turning it off, she listened. The melody was old and sweet, and she braced herself for the words that she knew would touch her soul.

The song was "Yesterday" by the Beatles. The words touched her as nothing ever had before. She began to gasp for air as the lyrics grasped at her very soul. The pain—how could she endure the pain ever growing inside her?

"Gabriella…" Blayne's eyes filled with tears. She didn't care who saw her and allowed them to fall down her face. She turned off the music. She closed her eyes and tried to find some peace in the darkness.

Elena pulled out an old box that had been put away years before. She opened it and allowed herself to look inside.

There were old photos and letters that had turned yellow with the passing of time wrapped in a pink ribbon. She opened a book of poetry by Jose Angel Buesa and gently touched the dried flowers folded within. Tears streamed down her face as she remembered all the promises made and all the promises broken.

"Mother, have you spoken to your attorney?" Chaz broke Abigail's concentration. She had been looking out at the garden. There were so many memories in the house. The children had grown up there. Arthur and she had spent most of their married life together there, as well. She needed good memories these days. She needed to hang on to something beautiful in view of the sadness that filled her every time she remembered that Arthur would soon be gone.

"Why?" She turned to face her son.

"Don't you think it would be wise...? I mean, Father is not in a good state of mind right now. And who knows what he might decide to do."

Abigail stared at her son in disbelief. "Your father would not cheat you, Chaz. I dare say he'll make provisions for Gabriella and her children, but you will certainly be well taken care of. And besides, darling, you have your own money that your father left you." Abigail tried to reassure him.

"How can you just allow this? I don't understand you, Mother. You just let his bastard stroll into this house!"

"Chaz! Your father is dying...please try to remember that," she said as her eyes filled with tears. She walked out of the room obviously distraught.

Chaz saw her leave and sat down in deep thought. Apparently, he was the only one this mattered to. He remembered how soft Gabriella felt when he took her in his arms. And who would have known what might have happened if Blayne hadn't stuck her nose where it didn't belong? She was always there before him. She was faster and smarter; she had all the things he wanted, even Gabriella. Had they? Yes, Blayne had probably already been in Gabriella's bed. The thought of that infuriated him. She always got there first. But this time, he would be the winner, no matter what it cost.

"You must be joking!" Blayne could not believe what she was hearing. "You can't honestly believe I would agree to this."

"Blayne, I want to try and settle as much as possible. At least he's showing some intent," Arthur argued.

She shook her head in disbelief as she sat behind her desk.

"Arthur…" She tried a different approach. "Where could I possibly put him so as to cause the least damage possible?"

"I want him at the headquarters. Make him one of your VPs. Give him a real chance."

"No!"

Arthur decided not to challenge her at this time. He had been doing everything wrong lately where Blayne was concerned, so he opted for caution.

"Why don't we talk about it when you get back?"

Blayne took a deep breath as she ran her fingers through her hair. "All right, all right."

"Diana tells me she's meeting you over there." Arthur changed the subject.

"Yes, we're going to try to spend some time together. At least that's the idea." Blayne laughed a little.

"Why do you laugh?" Arthur asked curiously.

"The last time Diana and I tried this, we ended up at the zoo, and you remember what happened then." She laughed harder.

Arthur laughed also. It had been so long since he had heard her laugh like that, and he realized how much Blayne had changed throughout the years.

"Yes, I remember. Diana decided she wanted a closer look at the monkeys and you ended up in the pond," Arthur reminded her.

"She was my responsibility. I had to get her out of there." Blayne laughed at the memory. Diana had always been... When had she lost that, she asked herself, and the laughter died in her.

Arthur seemed to be keeping pace with her emotions because at that moment he realized that she had seen the loneliness that had gradually taken hold, as well.

"Well, I promise no zoo this time."

"Keep your sister out of trouble."

"With Diana, there are no promises," she said distantly.

"Blayne..."

"Yes, Father?"

"I've always been so proud of you," he said. "You've always surpassed my expectations. I...I wanted you to know that."

Blayne felt the knot in her throat and tried to control the emotion from overwhelming her.

"I love you, Blayne." He could not control the emotion in his voice.

"I...I love you, too."

"It's great sailing weather today," he said, and as he did, his hand went out to her over the miles of ocean that separated them. "When you get back, we'll go out to the point. You loved going out there when you were a kid."

She could see the smile on his face without seeing him and she smiled, too. "Well, hard not to when you told me all those tales of sirens and Ulysses."

"Yes." He laughed. "When you get back then?"

"Yes, when I get back."

Arthur hung up and smiled to himself. Blayne had been such a beautiful child when he married Abigail. She was bright and vital. He remembered all the times they had gone out on the sailboat. It had become something that only they two shared, along with a love of history and his fascination with mythology. She had been a loving child, curious and a dreamer. It had been so easy to love her. He had gradually shaped her to one day take his place.

Arthur looked out into the ocean from his balcony and wished he had perhaps taught her other things, as well. He was proud of her. He couldn't have been prouder if he had fathered her himself.

He realized then that he should never have contacted Gabriella. Arthur finally saw the selfishness in that act. What had he expected? He only wanted to appease his conscience where Elena and Gabriella were concerned. He had not only hurt them, he realized, but he had mortally wounded Blayne. In this admission, he recognized his arrogance. He had yet again only thought of himself like he had done so many years earlier.

He didn't understand Blayne's desire, but he clearly saw the pain in her. Blayne had been able to hide things from the world, but he had always been able to read her eyes. She was his child. Blayne was the real child of his heart, and he had in his thoughtlessness destroyed her. Arthur's eyes filled with tears. He had been the one to break the heart of someone he loved yet again. Even now, he realized she was putting distance between herself and Gabriella. What had he done? Yet he knew that he had to make her understand that it was for the best.

He would do one thing for Blayne before his time was up; at least he would try to teach her a way of attaining some peace. The ocean had been his confessor, and in it, he had found some solace. In its vastness, he had found some sense of oneness. When Blayne got back, he would give her that. If nothing else, he would try to give her that.

It had been an incredibly harried morning. Chaz had been working as one of Blayne's VPs for the past two months, but she was glad to admit that no major disasters had come of it. Arthur was going through chemotherapy and seemed to be handling it better than expected. Abigail was fooling herself that he would get better and they all let her, knowing it was her way of dealing with the inevitable.

Blayne was so busy that there was no time left for her to give in to the bare facts of her present and the coldness to come of her future. Blayne was clearly a competent machine when she was focused. Her analytical mind took all in like a sponge, and the results were logical and mathematical equations; emotions had no place in her life. She worked best when she felt nothing, and lately, she seemed to do no wrong.

Diana waltzed into her office as she looked up irately at the interruption. Blayne was on an overseas call and motioned for Diana to sit.

Diana looked around the office and waited politely.

Blayne finally finished her call forty minutes later and turned toward her sister.

"Did we have an appointment?" Blayne asked curtly.

"Do I need one?" Diana said defensively.

Blayne was about to say something, then seemed to think better of it.

"All right, I'm sorry…I just meant…"

"You meant, how dare I interrupt you." Diana was clearly upset.

Blayne was about to argue, then just smiled.

"Yes." Her smile broadened. "I'm sorry. You're right. I was rude. Is there something I can help you with?"

Diana smiled at her sister. "That's better. No, I don't need anything. I just came to say hello and hopefully take you to lunch…"

The telephone interrupted them.

"I'm waiting for a call…give me a moment, okay?"

Diana nodded.

"Blayne Anberville."

"Blayne…"

Blayne froze. She seemed to stop breathing.

"I…I'm here in Boston. I need to see you." Gabriella's voice seemed to infiltrate every fiber of her body. Her eyes closed, trying to shut down the reaction.

"No" was all that came out of her mouth.

Diana noticed Blayne's demeanor immediately.

"I'm staying at the Copley Hotel…I'll be here only 'til morning. Blayne…come, please." Gabriella begged her softly.

"No." Blayne opened her eyes, and as soon as they focused and became aware of Diana, her body straightened. "I'm sorry that's not possible, goodbye," she said brusquely and hung up.

"You okay?" Diana searched her face. Blayne had gotten very pale.

"Yes…" Blayne looked down at her paperwork. "I'm sorry…but I won't be able to have lunch, I'm swamped." She looked up more in control of herself now.

"You look off keel. Sure you're okay?"

"I'm fine. Just really busy." She started shuffling papers around. "Maybe we can have lunch tomorrow if you're in town."

Diana smiled. "Actually, that's even better. Lunch tomorrow then at one, okay?"

"Yes, perfect. Where?" Blayne opened her appointment book to add it to her schedule.

"How about Sandrine's Bistro?"

"Great, I'll meet you there." Blayne made the note on her agenda and missed the totally devilish look that covered Diana's face.

Diana then got up happily. "Great! Well, I better let you get back to it."

Blayne smiled at her sister and nodded. That smile disappeared as the door closed behind Diana.

Gabriella is here... Her head fell back on the chair. *God, please...* Blayne closed her eyes in supplication.

Blayne found herself walking down a carpeted corridor that night. She stopped in front of a door and stared at the floor for a moment. Closing her eyes, she breathed in, then looked up, tèlling herself yet again that she was not going to give in to this...then she saw her hand go up and knock. Something inside her tore as she felt the pain of defeat.

The door burst open, and neither woman knew who had taken the first step toward the other. The connection of the senses overwhelmed and both inwardly breathed in a feeling of oneness that had escaped them for so long. Neither one wanted that moment to end. No words were spoken as mouths met desperately. Blayne moved forward and pushed the door closed behind her.

"Blayne...Blayne," Gabriella said over and over as Blayne's mouth traveled down her neck.

Blayne suddenly pushed her away from her at arm's length. She searched Gabriella's face. She wanted to remember every nuance of the woman who had haunted her every minute of every day and every long night. She wanted to burn that image forever in her mind and soul. Her hand reached out and touched Gabriella's face lightly.

A tear escaped Gabriella's eyes at the pain she saw on Blayne's face.

"I'm real…I'm here and I love you. Please…please let me love you." Tears ran down her face. "Tell me you still want me, please…"

Blayne closed her eyes and a whimper escaped her as she kissed Gabriella's lips. "Want you?" Blayne's pain was audible in every word as she spoke with her mouth touching Gabriella's lips. "I have never stopped wanting you… Gabriella, I'm dying for you." Her mouth then covered Gabriella's hungrily.

Words were not necessary…touches and caresses said it more profoundly than words could have. Their lovemaking was passionate one moment and slow and unrushed the next. It was a joining of something deeper. The union had become more than that of flesh, but of minds and souls. Their need was so palpable that there seemed no limit to the depth of the emotions and responses sought and exacted of each other. The need to feel one another was paramount to anything that might have or should have been said before. At the climax of their lovemaking, both screamed out and climbed even higher together. Never for one instant did either woman not touch the other.

Close to the dawn of a new day, they held each other covered under pristinely white sheets. Their breathing was steady, both knowing that the dawn would bring in the stark, cruel light of day. The night had cradled them protectively while the light of day would likely bring with it the ugliness of a truth neither wanted to face. Both clung to each other saying nothing, refusing to break the magic that held and bound them.

Gabriella closed her eyes and held Blayne tighter. Blayne was what she needed, what she wanted, and what could never be.

Blayne stared up at the ceiling as her arms pulled her lover closer to her. She leaned down and kissed Gabriella's head as tears escaped her eyes. Tonight, Gabriella was hers again, Blayne told herself, and tomorrow was a world away. If she were honest with herself, she would admit that she had known from the moment of the phone call that she would come. Blayne knew that the morning would bring recriminations and words that would hurt and cause pain. Both would seek an absolution in accusations and inevitably they would tear each other apart.

But at the moment, nothing mattered. Right here, right now, nothing mattered to either of them. The only thing that was important was those precious stolen hours. For those few hours, they had known the joy of oneness again. If only for a few hours, they had both been happy.

Chapter Ten

Blayne's eyes opened slowly. She smiled as the light of day verified that the woman who had filled her night was indeed in her arms that morning. Blayne's arms tightened around Gabriella as she pulled her closer. Her eyes closed in pain.

Every morning, Blayne woke smiling, her nights filled with dreams of the woman who had taken possession of her once cold and analytical mind only to be faced with the reality of her aloneness every morning as daylight taunted her. The light illuminated the darkness; it also made it abundantly clear that the oneness she felt in her dreams had only been that—a dream. The light brought to her the cruelty of her aloneness. But this morning was different.

Gabriella snuggled closer to Blayne as if knowing that her lover needed the warmth of her body. Her eyes fluttered opened, and she saw the turbulence in Blayne's.

Blayne could not hide her emotions. She was filled with need, want, and fear, all of which showed in her eyes. She was about to speak when Gabriella silenced her with a caress.

Gabriella touched her face lovingly and sensually, and as she did, her mouth came up to kiss the lips that called out to her.

Blayne didn't allow herself to think. Nothing mattered to her anymore. She no longer needed answers. Questions could wait. The truth of her reality no longer mattered to her; all she recognized and cared about was satisfying the ever-growing hunger to connect with the woman in her arms. Her desire to become one with Gabriella was undeniable and irresistible. Their joining was worth anything. It was worth everything.

So instead of questions and answers, there was only the need to satisfy the incredible longing that threatened to overcome them.

Much later, they held on to each other in silence. Both sated, enjoying the warmth that touching brought.

Nothing matters, Blayne told herself over and over. *Nothing matters.*

The ringing telephone cracked the fragile band that held them together. And like a thief, it stole the priceless gift.

Gabriella reached to answer it.

"Don't," Blayne's voice pleaded softly.

Gabriella turned to her. When she saw the tear-filled eyes of the woman in front of her, she felt the pain in her own chest. *The oneness is broken,* they communicated silently to each other. Gabriella went into Blayne's waiting embrace.

Blayne held her tightly as tears ran down her face.

"Blayne…" Gabriella began to say but was not allowed to continue.

"Don't…" Blayne again pleaded as she held her tighter still. "Not now…later."

Gabriella looked into the tear-filled eyes.

Again Blayne asked, "Later."

Gabriella nodded and kissed her lips. The telephone rang again. It continued to do so on and off for the next half-hour. Finally, Blayne's arms released her.

"It seems the world will not take no for an answer…" Blayne said, accepting the inevitable.

Gabriella sat up and picked up the ringing telephone.

117

S. Anne Gardner

"Hello?"

"Why didn't you answer? I've been calling you for at least twenty minutes. The hotel said you were in your room." Joseph sounded irate.

"I was taking a shower," Gabriella said. "Why are you calling?"

"Do I need a reason to call you?"

"Usually you do, yes."

There was silence between them for a moment, then Joseph picked up the conversation again in a conciliatory manner.

"Perhaps," he conceded. "We're all packed."

"Is all the flight information still the same?"

Blayne then sat up on the other side of the bed with her back to Gabriella.

"Yes, we're all confirmed."

"Good, then I'll meet you all at the airport this evening, and we can go on from there."

"All right. Elle is here and wants to talk to you."

"Okay, put her on." Gabriella ran her fingers through her hair and pulled the sheet up to cover her breasts.

The act did not go unnoticed by Blayne. The sheet became a visible wall. It was as real as the world that conspired to separate them.

"Mom?"

"Hello, Elle, how are you, sweetheart?"

"Okay. Do I have to go?"

"Yes."

"Why?"

"Elle, please…"

"Daddy says I have to act this way and that. I don't want to go!" the girl complained, and the usual strain that seemed to show of late was audible in her voice.

"Elle, you just be yourself."

118

"But Daddy…"

"Daddy is wrong. Just be you," Gabriella reassured. "You are a lovely young woman, just be you, honey."

Blayne got up and walked to the window naked.

Gabriella watched as she stood silently looking out.

"Elle, put Daddy on the phone."

"Okay, Mom, see you later."

"I love you, sweetheart."

"Love you, too. Here's Daddy."

"Hi," Joseph said as he got back on the phone.

"Joseph, she's nervous. This is hard for her. She's insecure enough. Just let it be, okay?" Gabriella said irately.

"I just asked her to behave," he said defensively.

"Just lighten up, okay? I'll see you all tonight."

"All right."

Gabriella hung up the phone and sat quietly for a moment with her back to Blayne.

"How's your family?" Blayne asked, breaking the silence.

"Elle and her father seem to clash over everything."

Both women still had not moved.

Blayne took a deep breath and dove in. "Why did you come?" She turned to face Gabriella.

"Because I need this as much if not more than you," she said as her eyes filled with tears that threatened to fall.

Blayne went to her immediately. She knelt in front of Gabriella and took her hands, holding them in hers with a desperation that frightened her. Gabriella kept staring at their hands.

"Stay with me," Blayne pleaded. "Please…on my knees….I beg you…please, stay with me…" she finished as she held back a sob.

Gabriella saw the tears running down Blayne's face. She could see the pain in those eyes that she so dearly loved.

"Stay with me…stay with me," Blayne asked yet again, unable to veil the desperation in her voice as she waited for an answer.

Gabriella's hand went out to caress the beautiful face. How could she tell her? How could she make her understand?

"I can't…" Gabriella's words cut Blayne through the heart. She visibly flinched, and an intake of breath from Blayne sounded like thunder to Gabriella's ears. She knew she had broken the heart that just a moment before had bared itself to her and begged her to stay and love her.

"Blayne…" Gabriella said when Blayne stood and put as much distance between them as possible. "Blayne, I can't…"

"You don't need to say anything. Words are overrated. No is quite sufficient," Blayne said coldly with her back to her.

"I wish I could…"

"Like hell you do!" Blayne said accusingly. "You got what you wanted. I fucked you and you got to fuck me." Blayne started picking up her clothes.

"It wasn't like that…"

"Wasn't it?" Blayne turned to her again.

"You know it wasn't." Gabriella met her eyes.

"What was it then? Love? You called me to come and fuck you in a hotel room, and you're meeting your children and …your husband!" Blayne growled as she pulled at the sheets.

Gabriella stood and covered herself with the sheet. Blayne walked up to her and pulled it off. "Ashamed of your nakedness? You weren't ashamed last night or this morning when we were *fucking*!"

"Stop it, Blayne, please," Gabriella pleaded as the tears filled her eyes again.

"Stop? Shouldn't you have said that last night?" Blayne

took a deep breath and released the woman who was now sobbing in front of her. "All right, all right…"

Blayne dressed quickly, and as she was about to leave, she stopped in front of the door, not daring to turn and face Gabriella, yet not able to just walk away. She had no shame, no pride left in her, and knowing it hurt her. She shut her eyes and said the words her soul wanted voiced and cursed herself for it. "Call me soon?"

"Yes," Gabriella said softly.

Blayne never turned. Her eyes shut again with the pain of the answer, then left the room. As Blayne walked out into the hallway, she pulled her sunglasses from her pocket and put them on. Her eyes were now shielded from the world.

She got on the elevator.

A woman got on before the elevator reached the lobby, and she admired the beautiful dark-haired woman with the sunglasses leaning on the corner. She also noticed as she exited the elevator how she proudly raised her chin as if preparing to face the world. The effect that Blayne caused with her looks was always that of aloof beauty and arrogance that came only with those that knew they were few and ruled the world. The woman blinked in surprise as the image she had in her mind of Blayne Anberville shattered when she saw the tears that escaped the veil of the sunglasses and roll down the beautiful cheek.

The effect Blayne left behind with the stranger was one of wonder and curiosity. *That could not have been Blayne Anberville. That cannot be the cold woman I've been told about. And yet it must be her.* Tara Montgomery shook her head and looked up again to see the figure disappear out of the hotel. *I look forward to meeting you more than ever now, Blayne, more than ever. Your tear has intrigued me. Perhaps this trip to Boston will be more than I hoped for.*

Tara smiled to herself and walked out of the hotel. She had shopping to do. After all, she had just found something that had awakened her, and she had to get just the right outfit to play the game.

Diana waited excitedly; she had gotten to the restaurant purposely early. Her face lit up with a smile as she got up and hugged her sister.

"I'm so glad we could do this," Diana said as she released Gabriella and they both sat down.

"It's good to see you, too, Diana. This place is wonderful," Gabriella said as she looked around.

"Sandrine's is wonderful. I always stop for lunch here when I'm in Boston. Raymond is a wonderful chef. You must try his famous Flammekeuche," Diana said enthusiastically.

"Flamm...what?" Gabriella laughed.

"Flammekeuche, it's a sort of pizza-quiche with bacon, onion, and lots of cream."

"Sounds wonderful. Do you know the chef?" Gabriella laughed. "You sound like a fan."

Diana joined in the laughter. "Yes, Raymond is a doll. He opened the restaurant a few years ago. Sandrine's is one of the little treasures of greater Boston."

"I love the décor," Gabriella said as she looked around. "The slate blues and hanging plates, it's lovely. Thanks for inviting me."

"I'm glad you came." Diana put her hand over her sister's and smiled.

The waitress appeared, and they ordered Cabernet-Sauvignon. The waitress went to get their wine order when Diana waved to someone behind Gabriella. She was beckoning her to their table.

"This is my surprise." Diana got up, and Gabriella turned to come face to face with Blayne, who was looking down on her with lifeless eyes.

Blayne walked into the restaurant and looked around the room. When she spotted her sister, she froze. The other woman sitting at the same table had her back to her, but she would recognize Gabriella anywhere, and a part of her hurt in knowing and acknowledging that. She took a deep breath and started walking toward Diana with a smile on her face. She, however, felt her resolve waiver when Gabriella turned and saw the unguarded look in those beautiful blue eyes.

"Hello, Gabriella," Blayne said politely and put her hand out.

Gabriella placed her hand in Blayne's silently.

"Oh, come on, you two, hug. We're all sisters."

Blayne held onto Gabriella's hand. Gabriella got up as if in a trance and went into Blayne's arms. She shut her eyes tightly and allowed her body to melt into the arms of the woman who had held her through the night.

Blayne broke the embrace by pulling away. "Hello, little sister."

Diana smiled.

Still facing Blayne, Gabrielle was about to speak when Blayne moved away to sit next to her. Gabriella took in a deep breath and turned with a smile on her face, as well.

"We just ordered some wine."

"I can't, I have a meeting after lunch," Blayne cut in.

"Okay, we were thinking of ordering the..." Diana began to say.

"The Flammekeuche?" Blayne said, looking at the menu.

Diana smiled indulgently. "Yes, you remembered."

"Of course," Blayne said, looking up. "You order it every time we meet here for lunch."

The waitress brought the wine and took the lunch order

S. Anne Gardner

from the three women. Gabriella had hardly said anything.

"What time are Joseph and the children arriving?" Diana asked.

Blayne's head looked up immediately. She waited, holding her breath.

"Ahh....they arrive at six thirty this evening," Gabriella said, not daring to look in Blayne's direction.

"I can hardly wait to see them. Blayne, you will absolutely love Elle and Christopher." Diana looked at Blayne now. She was surprised to see the expression on Blayne's face.

"Blayne?" Diana asked as Blayne only stared at Gabriella.

Gabriella focused on the tablecloth. Again, Diana didn't understand what was going on.

"Why are they coming here?" Blayne asked Gabriella, ignoring Diana.

Diana looked from Blayne to Gabriella, understanding less and less.

"Why?" Blayne asked again.

"They're coming to meet Daddy," Diana said.

Blayne looked toward Diana, then back to Gabriella, The disbelief, hurt, and coldness that showed in Blayne's eyes scared Gabriella.

Diana didn't like what she was seeing.

"I..." Gabriella began to speak, then looked back down at the tablecloth.

"I think it's very nice of Gabriella to do this for Daddy," Diana interjected.

Blayne continued to stare in disbelief, then turned her attention to the water glass in front of her. Diana could see the uncertainty and something else she could not understand going through Blayne's semblance. Her sister was growing pale, and Gabriella looked like she was about to bolt.

"I thought you guys liked each other," Diana said sadly.

Blayne and Gabriella remained silent.

"I want both my sisters to like each other," Diana murmured. "I'll need both of you when Daddy..." She trailed off.

Blayne put her hand over her sister's. "You won't be alone, Diana."

"I know." Diana looked up with eyes filled with tears. "I love both of you. I just want you two to remember that we're a family."

Blayne nodded.

Gabriella smiled and ran her hand along her sister's arm. "Yes, sweetheart," Gabriella said reassuringly.

Blayne looked up with such yearning at Gabriella. Gabriella was looking at Diana, but Diana saw it before Blayne released her hand and straightened up.

"Well, here comes our lunch." Blayne gave the waitress a brilliant smile.

All three sisters played at being polite throughout lunch. Diana seemed happy enough.

But the inevitable question arose as they finished lunch.

"Will you be coming tonight or tomorrow to the house?" Diana asked Blayne innocently.

Blayne saw the look of apprehension on Gabriella's face.

"I don't think so. I have to catch up on some things I put off yesterday," Blayne said with a touch of sarcasm.

"Couldn't you have arranged something?" Diana insisted.

"How could I since I didn't know?" Blayne sounded exasperated.

"I thought that Daddy...." Diana trailed off in confusion.

Blayne looked accusingly toward Gabriella, unable to hide her resentment.

"I'm sure he said he was going to tell you," Diana insisted.

"Perhaps it skipped his mind." Blayne began eating again. *Yeah, right. Nothing escapes Arthur. Damn this whole thing.* Blayne looked to Gabriella. *I hate you for putting me in this position. I hate myself more for letting you. I don't want to love you!* Blayne looked back at her food again as her thoughts kept invading her mind.

"Well, can't you try to get away for a little bit?" Diana wanted more than anything for Blayne and Gabriella to get along. She just didn't understand why they couldn't seem to get past whatever it was that had become a wall between them.

"No, I don't think so, sorry." Blayne tried to smile.

"It's okay. Blayne is busy. Perhaps another time?" Gabriella finally spoke.

"Yes, another time. When will you be coming back to Boston?" Blayne asked with a forced smile. She and Gabriella knew what she was asking.

"Soon. I promise," Gabriella said and looked down at her lunch.

"I'll hold you to that," Blayne added seriously.

Diana looked from one to the other.

Gabriella looked up and nodded. "Yes, soon. I promise."

Blayne turned and smiled so that Diana was pleased and Gabriella went back to her lunch.

Diana didn't understand them, and she wanted to desperately. Gabriella and Blayne made no sense to her at all. And Blayne was certainly not acting herself these days. Blayne had changed. Diana looked at her sister. Yes, something had changed in Blayne; she seemed sadder somehow.

She had noticed it after that day she found her on the

floor of her room weeping. And then she saw glimpses of it in London. Blayne's eyes were alert as they had always been, but there had been unguarded moments that Diana was taken aback by the incredible look of sadness.

In London, she had tried to talk to Blayne to no avail. Blayne wasn't talking and Diana knew instinctively that something inside of her was dying. Perhaps it had been the news about their father or even the shock of finding out about Gabriella, but somehow Diana didn't think so. Yes, those things had surprised them all, but there was something else happening inside Blayne, and it was taking its toll.

Blayne finally said her goodbyes and left the restaurant. Gabriella and Diana agreed to meet later at the house after she picked up her family at the airport.

Blayne and Gabriella seemed to be running, Diana thought to herself. She was not going to give up in getting her two sisters to get along. In a short period, she had begun to love Gabriella and her children. And she recognized that Blayne had been right. Whenever she called Gabriella, her sister made the time to talk to her, and she liked and needed that. Diana also knew that the closer she was getting to Gabriella, the distance between her and Blayne seemed to be growing.

Chapter Eleven

Blayne walked into her office and passed her secretary, Carla, without a word.

Carla walked in behind her and closed the door.

"Your three o'clock is here."

Blayne looked at the notes she had made on a file on her desk.

"Tara Montgomery, right?"

"Yes, she's here representing A.M.A.G. I put the file on your desk and the notes that you had made for this meeting. Is there anything else before I bring her in?"

"Just give me a few minutes." Blayne removed her jacket and looked through the notes.

"Yes, Ms. Anberville." Carla walked out, closing the door behind her.

A few minutes later, there was a small knock on the door and Carla showed in Tara Montgomery.

Blayne walked over to the woman and put her hand out. "Please come in, Ms. Montgomery. How are you? I'm..."

"You're Blayne Anberville," Tara said with a bright smile as she took Blayne's hand and held it. "The pleasure is mine, I assure you."

Blayne smiled and pointed to the chair in front of her desk. Tara looked around the office.

"Why don't we sit on your sofa instead? It'll make it more...cozy...don't you agree?" Tara asked charmingly.

Blayne was surprised but smiled and nodded. "If you like."

Tara sat and crossed her legs. She smiled when she caught Blayne looking at them.

"Let's talk business then, shall we, Ms. Anberville." Tara again gave Blayne a disarming smile.

Blayne could not believe what she thought she was seeing. The woman was openly flirting with her.

"Yes, of course, Ms. Montgomery. We want to…"

"Please, call me Tara." She put her hand on Blayne's leg.

"If you like."

"I like very much. Are you busy for dinner, Ms. Anberville?"

Chaz thought they were a gruesome circle at dinner. Joseph was obviously pleased to be there; he never stopped trying to engage and impress Arthur. Diana spoke amicably with Gabriella and her mother who seemed to be happy enough these days. The girl named Elle was brooding and the boy Christopher wouldn't stop talking to him.

"I don't have any other uncles," Christopher said to Chaz.

Chaz looked down at him, trying to control his obvious dislike.

"Yes, well, you have one now, don't you?"

"You have any other nephews?"

"No."

"Christopher, do you like horses?" Arthur asked his grandson, who smiled from ear to ear and nodded.

"If your parents are agreeable, maybe we can go riding tomorrow, would you like that?"

"Yes, Grandfather, that would be awesome."

Arthur and Abigail laughed at the boy's enthusiasm.

"How about you, Elena?"

"My name is Elle!"

Everyone's attention turned toward the moody child.

"I'm sorry, Elle," Arthur said conciliatorily.

"Elle, apologize this instant," Joseph insisted.

"Why?" the girl lashed out. "I didn't want to come."

"Elle!" Joseph stood.

"Joseph, leave it alone," Gabriella said angrily.

"It's all right. Elle has a right to demand to be called by her name." Arthur tried to intervene.

"Elle, apologize this instant," Joseph insisted.

Elle got more upset by the second. She didn't want all this attention. Everyone was staring. She got up and ran out of the room.

"You don't know when to stop, do you?" Gabriella said accusingly at Joseph as she went after her daughter. Joseph sat down and all conversation ceased at the dinner table.

Blayne was pulling into the driveway when someone ran in front of her car.

"Oh, my god!" She stopped abruptly and stared at the girl frozen in fear in front of her car.

Blayne got out and grabbed the girl harshly and turned her around to face her.

"What did you think you were doing?" Blayne shook from fear and so did Elle.

"Elle! Oh, my god, Elle!" Gabriella had seen the whole thing and ran toward them.

Blayne looked at the child in her grasp and stared at her as if looking at something foreign. She released the girl as soon as Gabriella reached them. Gabriella took Elle into her arms.

"My god, Elle, what were you thinking?" Gabriella was trembling with fear as she held her daughter tightly.

Blayne stared at mother and daughter. This was Gabriella's child. She met Gabriella's eyes for a moment before walking over to her car and getting in again.

Gabriella and Elle walked back inside as Blayne drove her Arnage T toward the garage area.

She looked at her hands and noticed how they shook when she got out of the car. She put them in her pockets and walked to the house.

When Blayne walked inside, they were all in the grand room having coffee. Arthur looked surprised and Diana smiled.

"Blayne." Diana walked over to her sister and hugged and kissed her.

Chaz smiled to himself and went to get a drink from the crystal decanter that had just been brought in.

Joseph stared at the woman in admiration and recognition.

"I'm so glad you came, Blayne." Diana walked her sister over to Gabriella and Joseph. "Come and meet Gabriella's family."

Gabriella seemed to pale and Elle leaned against a corner brooding. She didn't like the lady who had shaken her outside after almost running her over.

"Blayne, this is Joseph, Gabriella's husband." Diana made the introductions.

Joseph put his hand out. Blayne extended hers, as well.

"Hello," Blayne said politely.

"The pleasure is mine. I must admit the resemblance is uncanny, Gabriella," he said as he turned toward his wife.

"Excuse me?" Blayne said with her hand still in Joseph's.

He turned back to her again, still not releasing her.

"My wife has a bust of you in her studio."

Blayne pulled her hand out of his and looked at Gabriella who met her eyes. Gabriella broke the connection as she smiled and looked at her husband.

Diana jumped in, trying to break the awkward silence that fell between them. "Well, perhaps when it's done, you'll let us see it. I don't think I saw it when I was at your home."

"Gabriella is very private about her work. I think I got a preview because I surprised her one afternoon." Joseph stared at his wife.

Arthur walked over. "Blayne, how wonderful that you could make it."

Blayne turned toward Arthur, and he could see that she was angry at him.

"Hello, Father," she greeted him politely.

"Well, well, well, the whole family together," Chaz said as he poured himself yet another drink. "This is going to be a very interesting weekend. Don't you think so, Blayne?" Chaz taunted.

"Chaz, I can see that you're the same boar as ever," Blayne challenged.

"Where will you be sleeping tonight?" Chaz asked venomously.

"All right, you two, don't start up." Abigail slid her arms into Chaz's arm. "Whatever are you talking about?"

"Chaz!" Arthur intervened.

"Still brooding because I knocked you on your ass, Chaz?" Blayne taunted back.

"Enough, you two!" Arthur jumped in. He wanted the situation controlled.

Joseph just stared from one to the other not understanding a thing. Diana noticed how Gabriella paled and tried holding her hands to stop their shaking.

"Be good, Chaz," Abigail implored.

"Yes, Mother." He gave her a charming smile. "Blayne's

a big girl after all, isn't she?"

"And ever more successful at it than you." Blayne couldn't stop herself.

"Chaz! Not another word. Blayne, that's enough. Do you really want to pursue this here and now?" Arthur asked.

Blayne looked around and saw the face of the girl and the young boy staring at her curiously. She shook her head and walked away toward the crystal decanters and poured herself a drink.

"Good." Arthur took a deep breath. "You must pardon these two, Joseph."

Joseph smiled at Arthur. "I understand, Arthur. My sister and I are the same. We never stop competing." Joseph smiled.

Blayne turned to him with a smile of disgust. Gabriella did not fail to notice.

"Blayne, come here and meet the children," Diana said as she took her sister by the arm. "What the hell is going on between you and Chaz these days?" she asked under her breath as they walked toward Christopher first.

"This is Christopher," Diana said with a smile.

Blayne smiled and put her hand out to the handsome boy.

"Yeah, that's me."

"You're taller than I imagined," Blayne said.

The boy smiled proudly. "Grandfather is taking me riding tomorrow." The excitement was evident in his voice.

"Is he now? Are you a good rider, young man?" Blayne was enjoying talking to the boy. Diana walked away, leaving them in an animated conversation. She also noticed that Gabriella would turn every so often and look toward Blayne.

Elle remained separate and apart. Gabriella went over to her daughter.

"Do you want to go to bed, sweetheart? Are you sure you weren't hurt?"

"I'm okay," Elle said, frowning toward Blayne. "Who is she, Mom?"

Gabriella looked toward Blayne who was now talking with Abigail and Christopher.

"She's Abigail's daughter and Diana's sister."

"Is she your sister, too, then?"

"No," Gabriella answered, still looking at Blayne.

Elle looked toward her mother now. "I saw the bust of her in your studio."

Gabriella smiled and looked at her daughter. "Did you?"

"She looks different in real person, though. You made her look...I don't know, she seemed different."

Gabriella smiled secretly to herself and looked back at Blayne, and this time Blayne looked back at her. For a moment, both just looked at each other, basking in the memories, if only for a second or two.

"Elle, are you going riding tomorrow, as well?" Chaz's words next to her broke her contact with Blayne and Gabriella looked from Chaz to her daughter.

"I guess."

"I shall pick out a special pony for you tomorrow then," Chaz said charmingly.

The evening dragged on until finally Gabriella excused herself and left to put the children to bed. The other adults remained over their coffee and drinks.

Blayne had just gotten into bed when she heard a soft knock on her door. She frowned, thinking it was Chaz for another round of taunting. She yanked the door open.

"What do you want?"

She went silent when she saw Gabriella standing in front

of her. Gabriella walked in passed her.

Blayne closed the door and turned to her in disbelief.

"What do you think you're doing?"

"I don't know. Why did you come?"

"How could you bring him here?" Blayne asked as she got closer. The betrayal she felt was evident in her words.

"I...I promised Arthur that he could see the children," Gabriella said lamely.

"You brought him here!" Blayne spat out the words in disgust.

"I want you."

"I can't believe I've let this happen." Blayne turned away from her and ran her fingers through her hair. She felt tired and beaten. She closed her eyes and just wanted the ground to open up and swallow her whole.

"I want you. I don't love him," Gabriella insisted as she reached for Blayne.

"But you go to him!" Blayne snarled at her. "You go to him."

"I'm right here." Gabriella closed the distance between them. "I'm right here with you."

Blayne pushed her away. "Sure, long enough to pacify me and to go back to his bed." Blayne covered her face for a moment and felt the desperation building in her. "I can't do this. I can't."

"Blayne..."

Blayne stared as Gabriella opened her robe and let it fall to the floor. "I'm yours, my darling. I'm here and I'm yours."

Blayne shook her head as Gabriella approached her. "No..."

"I belong to you, Blayne." Gabriella pressed herself against Blayne and caressed her face. "I belong to you."

Blayne's mouth trembled as she felt Gabriella's hand

behind her neck, pulling her mouth closer. Blayne's eyes closed at the instant of that union. Her arms came up and pulled Gabriella tightly to her.

In the early hours of the morning, Gabriella left Blayne's room. She closed the door behind her, ran her fingers through her hair, and straightened her robe as she walked down the hallway into her room.

Diana had woken up with a headache and gone down to the kitchen for a warm glass of milk. On her way back to her room, she saw Gabriella walking out of Blayne's room and for some reason remained silent. She stood frozen in the spot and didn't understand. Blayne must obviously be up, so she walked over to her door and let herself in without knocking. She wanted to make sure her two sisters hadn't had another fight.

"I knew you would come back," Blayne said from the bathroom. The door was ajar. "Come on and take a shower with me. I promise to be good." Blayne walked out of the bathroom naked with a sultry smile on her face that disappeared the minute she came face to face with Diana. Both women stared at each other without being able to utter a word.

Diane seemed confused and walked out of the room quickly unable to look Blayne in the eye. Blayne stood frozen by the door frame unable to breathe.

Oh, my God! Oh, my God! Diana kept saying to herself over and over. She walked into her room and closed the door behind her. She took in a deep breath and leaned back. Diana needed to feel something solid behind her because she was sure she would just collapse. *I must be wrong. I just misread it all.*

She shook her head as if to dispel what she knew to be

the truth.

Oh, my God!

Diana walked over to the bed and sat looking straight ahead in utter shock.

Blayne and Gabriella are... She shook her head again.

She got up and started pacing.

Oh, my God!

Diana walked down to breakfast wondering how she was going to face Blayne and Gabriella. She walked into the dining room and saw almost everyone serving themselves.

"Good morning, darling," Abigail said, and Diana smiled.

She looked around and noticed that Blayne was not down yet. Gabriella was helping Christopher get some eggs from the serving tray.

Gabriella looked in her direction and smiled at her, then turned toward her son again.

Blayne walked in. Diana went over to the buffet and started serving herself breakfast.

"Good morning, Diana." Gabriella went to pour some orange juice next to her sister.

Diana was silent and didn't answer.

"Are you okay?" Gabriella asked, concern evident in her voice.

Diana looked at her and searched her face.

"I didn't sleep well," Diana said. "How about you?"

Gabriella seemed confused. "I slept just fine."

"Did you?"

"Yes."

"Diana," Blayne said behind her.

"I saw you this morning," Diana said, still looking at Gabriella, ignoring Blayne.

"Diana," Blayne insisted.

137

"I don't understand," Gabriella said, looking from Diana to Blayne.

"I saw you" was all that Diana kept saying.

"Diana, let me talk to you." Blayne tried to redirect the conversation. "Diana, please, not here."

"I saw you leaving Blayne's room this morning." Diana saw the confirmation she needed in Gabriella's face.

"I...yes, I went to talk to Blayne early this morning," Gabriella said.

"Too bad you couldn't stay for the shower," Diana blurted out.

Gabriella became paler. Blayne pleaded with her sister. "Diana, it's not what you think, please, not here."

Diana looked around and nodded. She walked away from them, sat at the table, and talked to Elle. Blayne stood in front of Gabriella shielding her from the others as she spoke to her.

"I'll talk to her." Blayne tried to give Gabriella the courage not to fall apart.

"How? How did she..." Gabriella muttered in a daze.

"She walked in after you left, and I said some things from the bathroom...I thought it was you, and I walked out naked." Blayne looked down.

"It's not your fault."

Blayne looked up and her eyes expressed the pain she feared to voice.

"This was not your fault. We'll figure something out," Gabriella said compassionately. She felt guilty enough about Blayne already without laying this on her, as well.

"I'll try and get her away from everyone after breakfast. Diana tends to act out when she's confused." Blayne stared at Gabriella. "I need to know that you'll be here if..."

"There will be no if...we have to fix this," Gabriella said nervously. "Joseph will take my children away from me,

Blayne. There can be no ifs."

"No, there can't, can there?" Blayne said sadly and walked over and sat next to Diana.

Little was said by any of the three women over breakfast. Gabriella kept looking at Diana, but Blayne seemed depressed and didn't look at her.

When breakfast was finished, Gabriella noticed when Diana and Blayne walked out together. She took a deep breath and began to breathe easier.

Chapter Twelve

"I thought I knew you." Diana peeled the petals off a flower she had plucked from the garden.

"You do know me," Blayne said sadly.

Diana looked up to meet her sister's eyes. "Why didn't you ever tell me?"

Blayne took a few steps away and ran her fingers through her hair before she sat down on a bench nearby.

"Tell you what? That Gabriella and I...? That's not exactly something that..." Blayne just trailed off.

"Yes, that and the fact that you're obviously interested in women." Diana sat next to her. "Why didn't you trust me? I know I'm not exactly what you would want in a sister, but I would have kept your secret."

Blayne saw the hurt in Diana's eyes. "You're the only sister I have and the only one I would want. I didn't tell you because there was nothing to tell." Blayne took a deep breath. "I mean, I...yes, I have been attracted to women off and on in the past, but nothing ever came of it." Blayne stood up nervously. "With Gabriella, it was something I just couldn't...."

"You just couldn't what? Did she?"

"No!" Blayne turned toward her sister. "I mean, I'm the one that..." Blayne couldn't find the right words.

Diana waited patiently.

"I couldn't stay away from her," Blayne said as she

lowered her head. "I didn't give her a chance to think, and I don't think I even gave her a chance to take a deep breath. I need her, Diana."

Diana stared at her usually controlled sister and saw the same thing she had seen that day she found Blayne crying on the floor in her room. Diana saw the desperation clearly in Blayne's demeanor, and she could hear it in her voice.

"That day!" Diana said.

Blayne looked at her now with tear-filled eyes.

"That day you were so upset and I found you…that day you and her?"

Blayne nodded. "I love her, Diana. I need her so much I have no power to stop myself. All she has to do is call and I go running," Blayne said shamefully.

"Does she love you?"

"I don't know. She says she does. I think she does." Blayne voiced the insecurities that tormented her soul. "I don't think she really knows."

"You have to walk away from this. It can't end well, you must see that." Diana was the voice of reason that she didn't want to hear.

"I can't," Blayne said in resignation as she got up. "Will you keep our secret?" Blayne waited patiently for an answer.

Diana saw Blayne differently now. She saw the strain that was visible in the usually confident semblance. She also saw the stress and the need for understanding in Blayne's eyes. Blayne had always been there no matter what; she couldn't just bail out on her now.

Diana nodded and Blayne visibly relaxed.

"Thank you."

Blayne walked back into the house and Gabriella immediately locked gazes with her. Blayne nodded and

Gabriella smiled and turned to continue speaking with Abigail. Diana noticed the silent communication and saw her sister walk out of the room. Blayne walked as if she had the weight of the world on her shoulders and Diana frowned.

Diana walked over to Gabriella when she saw that Abigail had gone to speak with Joseph and Elle.

"I don't like what you're doing," Diana said to Gabriella point blank.

Gabriella's chin stuck out. "This is not your concern, Diana. Blayne and I are adults."

"You'll end up destroying her, and she'll let you because she loves you," Diana said angrily.

"I love her, too. I don't want to hurt her."

"Do you? Do you love her, Gabriella?"

"Yes, I do."

"Then leave her alone."

"I can't."

Diana took a deep breath. "People thought that just because Blayne was so sure of herself and so smart that she had no feelings to hurt. When she was in high school, she was the valedictorian, at college, she excelled in everything. Her intelligence has always separated her from people. They all saw her as just a highly developed thing that could brilliantly solve any solution, and usually did, with no feelings to hurt. But I saw her disappointments when she failed the limits she set for herself. I was the one that would sneak in her room and hear her cry herself to sleep."

Diana looked at Gabriella and saw the tears building in her eyes, then she said the thing she knew would strike a blow. "And I held her as she sobbed that day when you were here last. What did you say to her then? Did you use her and just walk away?"

Gabriella's lips trembled and Diana realized that was exactly what must have happened.

"You're the only person that can really hurt her. I can see that." Diana tried to appeal to the woman she thought her sister to be. "You have reached inside her. Blayne is the best of us. She's better than all of us put together. She's something fine and noble. They don't make them like her anymore. You have obviously taken something precious from her by making her your lover. Will you leave your husband for her? Or will you just keep her around as your whore?" Diana saw the shock register in Gabriella's eyes. "Don't kill her spirit. She'll never recover from that."

Gabriella took a step back and away from Diana. She covered her mouth at the horror of the words. Diana had voiced the truth, and all she could do was walk away. She couldn't even be angry because ultimately she had to recognize that Diana was right. She had used Blayne without any thought. All she had thought about was her need, not Blayne's. Suddenly, the room made her feel closed in and she fled very much the same way Blayne had minutes earlier.

Gabriella instinctively knew where Blayne would be. She opened the door to the library and saw the woman she was looking for deep in thought standing by the window looking over the lawn. Gabriella walked up behind her and put her hands through Blayne's arms and around her stomach and pulled her to her, taking in a deep breath. Blayne's body recognized her immediately and allowed herself to lean back and feel the woman she loved envelop her in the intimate embrace.

"How I needed to feel your arms around me, my love," Blayne said breathlessly as she wrapped her arms around Gabriella's. "Gabriella, I love you. God, how I love you."

Gabriella kissed the side of Blayne's face. "As I love you."

"What are we going to do? I can't let you go." The

desperation came through in Blayne's voice.

"We have to be careful. No one can suspect."

Blayne turned around and searched Gabriella's face. "How long do you think we can get away with this?" she asked in disbelief.

"No one can know. I can't risk losing my children. You know this."

"I don't want that. But you have to see that this…this is not enough. When will we see each other again? In a week? A month? Two months?"

"I don't know." Gabriella turned her back to her.

"Don't you want to see me?" Blayne could hear how pitiful she must sound.

Gabriella faced her again. "You know I do. Surely, you know how I feel. I love you. I love you, I do."

"Not enough to stay with me," Blayne said angrily.

"I want to be, but I can't."

"Can you honestly tell me that this arrangement is enough for you?" Blayne waited.

"For now, it must be."

"For now?"

"Yes, for now."

"And when will it change?"

"I don't know," Gabriella said in exasperation.

"What am I to you?"

"What do you mean?"

"What am I?"

"You're the one I love."

"The one you *fuck*," Blayne said coldly.

"Yes, fine, the one I fuck!" The minute she said the words, she regretted it.

Blayne left the room before Gabriella could speak. "No, you're my love," Gabriella whispered to herself as she cried in earnest.

144

Arthur saw as Blayne ran out of the library like the devil was chasing her. He turned toward the library and went inside. Instinctively, he knew that Gabriella would be there.

He walked in and saw Gabriella crying. Arthur touched her shoulder gently. She turned to him with tears running down her beautiful face. The understanding and sadness she saw in his eyes was more than she could take, and the walls that kept her controlled emotions confined fell apart.

Gabriella went into his open arms and wept as he held her tightly. Arthur stroked her hair, trying to console her. This was the first time he held his daughter.

"Why can't she see that I need her as much as she needs me?" Gabriella sobbed in her father's shoulder.

Arthur stiffened for a moment and understood what must have occurred.

"Blayne sees things perhaps too clearly sometimes. She never sees the obstacles, just what is needed, and sets a path." He said sadly.

Gabriella pulled away from him and wrapped her arms around herself.

Arthur watched her as she took a few paces away and seemed to stare in front of her.

"She doesn't understand that what we want just can't be." Gabriella voiced the sadness she felt overwhelming her soul.

He just listened, not voicing his thoughts on the matter. This was the first time his daughter had reached out to him.

"I hurt her. I said such an ugly thing to her." Gabriella covered her mouth to control the sobbing. "God I hurt her."

Arthur put his arms around her, and she turned and buried her face in his chest.

"How could I hurt her like that?" Gabriella cried.

Elle had walked out, looking for a quiet place. She didn't like being in that house with all those people. They didn't like her and she didn't like them. Her Aunt Diana seemed nice enough, but she wasn't too crazy about Chaz. The man who was her grandfather seemed okay, but she didn't really know him. And Blayne she was sure she didn't like at all. After she had almost run her over, she had scared her half to death.

Elle wandered into the garages behind the house. She saw cars that she didn't recognize, but what caught her attention was the restored Harley-Davidson in one corner. There were a few other motorcycles, but the Harley left her speechless. Elle walked around it admiring the big machine. It was the most impressive bike she had ever seen. Her fingers went out to touch it.

"Don't touch that!" Blayne shouted.

Elle jumped in fear and withdrew her hand. She took a step back upon seeing the eyes filled with anger directed toward her.

"I'm sorry…" Elle was about to walk away when Blayne put her hand on Elle's shoulder.

Elle turned toward Blayne with her face down in submission.

"Look at me," Blayne said in a softer tone.

The child raised her head defiantly with a frown on her face.

Blayne smiled. "That's better. Never allow anyone to bully you."

Blayne turned and began walking away, leaving the child with a confused and curious look on her face.

"I don't like you!" Elle yelled.

Blayne stopped and turned around. "That's your right." Blayne began walking away again. "I'm going to take out the Harley in about an hour. If your mom lets you, I'll give you a ride and you can see how she handles."

Blayne did not wait for a reply and continued walking away as a smile appeared on her face.

Elle watched her, not understanding whether she wanted to like her or not. She thought about whether she should go for a ride on the Harley with Blayne. The child looked toward the bike in admiration; she hesitated only for a moment, then took off running to ask her mother's permission.

"Mom!" Elle was yelling as she entered the house.

Gabriella went out of the library seeking her daughter.

"Elle? Are you all right?" Gabriella held onto her daughter's shoulder.

Elle was trying to catch her breath. "Mom…"

"Honey, just take a deep breath…are you okay?"

"Mom, can I go for a ride on her bike? Please, Mom… please."

"Elle, what are you talking about?"

Arthur walked out of the library and smiled at his excited granddaughter.

"Please, Mom…please!" Elle insisted.

"Elle, what are you talking about?"

"I think she's talking about Blayne's bike, right?" Arthur joined them.

"Yes, it's incredible. She says if you say it's okay, she'll give me a ride. Please, Mom, please!" Elle began all over again, looking at her mother and pulling at her arm.

"What do you mean a bike?" Gabriella asked suspiciously. "As in a motorcycle?"

Elle nodded with a big smile on her face.

"Please, Mom, oh, please."

"Elle, I don't think so. It's not safe." Gabriella hated denying her daughter the pleasure she saw in her face. Elle rarely expressed such interest in anything these days.

Immediately, the child looked forlorn. Blayne was coming down the staircase, and Gabriella watched her walk leisurely. She was wearing tight black leather pants and a jacket. Blayne seemed like something wild and untamable, and she forgot to tell herself that she must hide what she wanted to do to the woman coming down the staircase. Blayne's eyes never left hers.

Elle looked toward the staircase sadly.

Blayne walked up to the small group. "My father will tell you that I have never had an accident on the bikes."

Elle looked from Blayne to her mother. "Please, Mom."

"No."

Elle took off running.

"Elle! Elle, wait." Gabriella went after her daughter.

"I didn't mean to…" Blayne said as she stared after Gabriella.

"Gabriella is very protective of her daughter. The child is very withdrawn," Arthur said.

"She's just afraid," Blayne said distractedly as she stared after mother and child.

"What is she afraid of?" Arthur looked at Blayne with curiosity.

"Everything, she's thirteen." Blayne still stared at the door that Elle and Gabriella had run out of.

"Blayne…?"

Blayne faced her father. "Yes?"

"Are you all right?" Arthur touched his daughter's arm.

Blayne looked down, then met his eyes again. "What is all right?"

"Blayne…"

"No…" Blayne said as she walked out of the house.

"Elle?" Gabriella walked up to her daughter.

"I don't fit in anywhere…" Elle sobbed. "I want to go

home."

"Elle…come here, baby." Gabriella reached out to her daughter.

The girl turned away, then suddenly ran into her mother's embrace and cried even harder.

"Elle." Gabriella caressed her daughter's hair and kissed her head. The roar of the motorcycle got Gabriella's attention. Blayne was pulling out of the garage and stopped looking at her.

Gabriella smiled and raised her daughter's face. "Go… listen to what Blayne tells you."

Elle's features were instantly filled with joy. She kissed her mother and ran toward Blayne.

Blayne got off the bike and helped Elle with her helmet. She then got back on and helped the girl climb in behind her. Before pulling out, Blayne looked at Gabriella for a moment, then the bike and its two riders pulled out of the driveway.

"It's a nice bike," Elle said, sitting next to Blayne on the grass. They had stopped after they had ridden for a good hour.

"Thanks. You like it, huh?"

"Yeah, it's awesome."

Blayne couldn't help but smile at the excitement emanating from the girl.

"What grade are you in?" Blayne asked, looking at the horizon.

Elle took a deep breath and looked from Blayne to the horizon, as well. "I'll be starting high school in the fall."

"Scared?"

Elle was about to give her usual smart mouth answer when she looked at Blayne. She realized that Blayne was really asking her. She wasn't laughing at her or staring like most people did when she told them.

"Yeah." Elle looked down at her feet.

"You can tell your mom you don't want to go, and she'll understand." Blayne turned to look at Elle now.

"My dad will get mad. He made all the arrangements." Elle got up and took a few steps away and turned her back to Blayne. "They fight a lot. I don't want them to fight because of me."

"I'm sorry."

Elle nodded. "My mom likes you."

It was Blayne's turn to stare at the ground as Elle turned around to face her.

"I saw the bust of you." Elle waited to see Blayne's eyes rise to meet hers.

"Yeah?"

"Yeah…that's how I know she likes you," Elle said seriously.

Blayne's head turned to the side. "I went to high school when I was thirteen, too."

"Did you hate it?" Elle asked.

"Yeah." Blayne kicked the ground with her boot, then she got up, as well. "Why do you hate it?"

"I won't know anyone. All the kids will make fun of me."

Blayne turned sad eyes toward the girl. She knew the pain of being different only too well.

"Talk to your mom," Blayne said again. "She'll understand."

"Maybe."

"Come on, let's go before your mother thinks I've kidnapped you."

Elle looked at Blayne, and they both laughed.

"You let her what?" Joseph could not believe what he was hearing.

"Blayne will take good care of her," Gabriella said.

"What is happening with you? We have always thought that motorcycles are dangerous. I can't believe you allowed it." Joseph walked away from her furious.

Gabriella sat on the bench. Why had she allowed it? Because Elle had seemed happy and happy was not something Elle had been for a long time. She desperately wanted to reach her daughter. It had been such a long time since she understood what her girl needed. She was losing Elle and she knew it. Joseph was just too blind to admit it. Elle had an incredible mind, but where once it was filled with curiosity and wonder, these days all Elle seemed to be was sad and depressed.

"Mom, Grandpa and I are going to go fishing, want to come?"

Gabriella noticed Christopher next to her and smiled. "I'm sorry, sweetheart, I didn't hear you."

"Want to come fishing with Grandpa and me?"

Gabriella smiled and looked up at Arthur who seemed pale.

"Are you feeling all right?" Gabriella asked as she got up.

"Yes, I'll be fine. I'm going fishing with my grandson."

Gabriella saw the sadness hidden behind the smile. He wanted to spend as much time with his grandchildren as possible. Time was the only thing he didn't have.

Gabriella nodded sadly. "Don't stay out too long."

Arthur smiled and nodded. "Come on, Christopher. Have I told you about the trout I caught at your age?"

"How big was it?"

Gabriella smiled sadly as she watched them walking away.

"I don't know how you two think you're going to pull

this off," Chaz said mockingly as he walked up to Gabriella in the garden.

She looked up to the sky and back down again in exasperation before she turned to Chaz.

"Whatever are you talking about, Chaz?"

"You and my sister." He bit into an apple. Chaz seemed relaxed and handsome as usual. How he could say such insensitive things, yet manage to look like it was just light conversation Gabriella would never understand. What seemed to disarm her about Chaz constantly was how much he looked like Blayne; there of course is where the resemblance stopped.

"I still don't know what you're talking about."

"Okay, keep playing your little games. I just hope I'm around when it blows up in your faces." Chaz laughed loudly.

"Chaz, are you behaving yourself?" Diana asked, suddenly standing next to both of them.

"Me?" he asked incredulously. "You mean our sister, don't you?"

"Chaz, you're being a boar again."

"Fine, look the other way if you want to." Chaz walked away from them.

"Are you all right?" Diana asked Gabriella.

"Chaz is someone I won't miss when I leave here."

"That's not what I meant." Diana sat on the bench. "I love you both, you know."

Gabriella smiled and sat next to her sister. "I know." She had known exactly what Diana meant.

"What are you going to do?"

"I don't know." Gabriella was about to say something when she heard the roar of the motorcycle pulling into the driveway. "Blayne and Elle are back." Gabriella got up.

"Gabriella?" Diana reached out for her sister's hand.

"Yes?"

Joseph was walking toward them. Diana released her sister's hand. "I think Joseph is angry."

Gabriella turned toward her husband as Elle and Blayne were walking toward her and Diana.

"Elle, go inside," Joseph instructed.

Elle looked up at Blayne who nodded. She then looked at her mother, who caressed her face and smiled at her. "Go on, sweetheart. You can tell me all about your ride later."

Elle walked in the house.

"I don't want my daughter riding a motorcycle," Joseph said harshly at Blayne, whose face became cold as steel.

"Joseph, I gave her permission," Gabriella intervened.

"You made a mistake. I don't want Elle on a motorcycle."

Diana wanted to disappear. She was becoming more nervous by the second as she saw the expression on Blayne's face.

"You don't make all the decisions where the children are concerned. Elle was actually happy. Didn't you notice? When was the last time she seemed happy to you?"

"A lot of difference that would make if she were dead!"

The noise of the slap to his face left everyone in shock.

"Don't you ever say that! Never say that!" Gabriella was yelling.

Joseph stared at her as if she had lost her mind. "What's the matter with you these days?"

"Don't you say that my baby will die. Don't you dare say that ever!" Gabriella began crying in earnest.

Joseph stared in disbelief. "I didn't mean it like that. I…"

"I love her. I would never intentionally put her in harm's way." Gabriella turned her back to him and continued to weep.

"I know that...I didn't mean to..." Joseph seemed genuinely sorry.

Blayne stared at them and realized there was something more going on than just her taking Elle for a ride.

Joseph tried putting his arms around his wife. Gabriella pulled away from him. "Don't!"

"Gabriella, I said I was sorry." He tried getting closer to her again.

Blayne stared, not understanding what was happening.

"Don't touch me!"

Joseph's hands suddenly lowered. He took a deep breath and spoke softly to her. "I never blamed you. I swear I never blamed you."

Gabriella looked away.

"I loved her, too. It wasn't anyone's fault," Joseph said, then walked away.

Blayne looked at Diana and saw the same question in her eyes.

Gabriella looked at Blayne with tear-filled eyes. Blayne stared back, then walked away, as well. She wasn't about to give Gabriella a chance to hurt her again if she could help it.

Gabriella closed her eyes as tears escaped them.

"She's hurt." Diana tried to console Gabriella, who seemed even more upset as she watched Blayne walk away.

"Yes, I know. I hurt her." Gabriella turned and walked toward the house, as well.

Dinner was a solemn affair. Elle kept looking up from her father to her mother who barely spoke. Christopher was the only one talking excitedly about his adventures while fishing with his grandfather.

"I wish you could all stay longer," Arthur said to

Gabriella.

"The children have school."

Joseph was about to speak, then Gabriella added, "I also have meetings scheduled with the gallery for my upcoming exhibition."

Blayne looked up but said nothing.

"You'll let me know when and where?" Diana asked. She wanted Gabriella to know that although she didn't approve of her relationship with Blayne, they were still sisters.

Gabriella smiled at Diana and nodded.

"Are you and Blayne taking the sailboat out tomorrow?" Abigail asked Arthur. "Perhaps the others would like to go, too."

Elle looked up immediately. "Mom?"

Gabriella smiled indulgently at her daughter and nodded.

"Why don't you go with her? I'll stay with Christopher." Joseph turned to Arthur to explain. "Christopher gets seasick."

"I get seasick, too...I'll wait here on land." Diana laughed.

Arthur laughed, too, remembering the last time he had taken Diana out on the boat and the disastrous outcome.

"What time are we going?" Elle asked excitedly.

"We sail at nine a.m. Have you sailed before?" Arthur was pleased to have finally been able to engage his granddaughter in conversation.

"No, not really. Will we go out far?"

"Blayne and I usually go out to a nearby island. We'll be gone most of the day." Arthur was pleased. He turned toward his daughter and surprised Gabriella and Blayne. "Come with us, Gabriella."

"Yes, darling, why don't you?" Joseph encouraged her.

"Perhaps she doesn't like sailing," Blayne said curtly

as she looked up, challenging Gabriella to argue with her. She knew she was annoying Joseph, but she didn't care; she wanted as much distance as possible between Gabriella and herself.

"Yes, why don't you?" Chaz said, enjoying the discomfort.

"Please, Mom...come with us," Elle said.

Gabriella looked at Blayne, then smiled at Elle and nodded.

After the coffee was served, Blayne excused herself, saying she had calls to make.

Gabriella had tucked the children into bed and was changing when Joseph came up behind her and tried taking her in his arms. She immediately walked away from him.

"Please don't," she said as she pulled her robe closed.

"We have to talk about this."

"There's nothing to talk about," she said and began to fidget.

He knew only too well the signs of her reaction. The doctor had said it would take time. But it had been a year already, and nothing seemed to change. If anything, things had gotten worse in the last few months.

"I think we should go to therapy together," Joseph said.

"Why bother...?"

He stared at her for a moment before speaking. "Because a marriage includes sex with your husband."

She turned to him and searched his face. "Do you love me, Joseph?"

"How can you ask?"

"Do you love me?"

He looked at her and took a few steps away, then faced her again. "Yes, I love you."

"I don't think you do," she said sadly.

"We've had a few bad times, but all couples do. But yes, Gabriella, I love you very much. I'm sorry if you've ever doubted that," he said, taking a step closer to her.

Gabriella turned her back to him. "I'm sorry, Joseph," she said as she walked toward the door.

"Did you ever love me?

She turned to look at him sadly. "Yes, once upon a time when we were just two dumb kids." Tears escaped her eyes. "I did love you once before you hurt me…I thought you were the one…but you weren't. You said all the right things, but it all turned out wrong."

"What went wrong? What changed?"

"We did. We were a mistake. I expected too much and you got too little."

"I'm sorry about so many things. We can try again, can't we?" Joseph walked closer. "I can be that man you loved once."

"I can't be with you." Gabriella began to breathe nervously. "I can't."

"Will you at least try counseling? I think if we resolved what happened with the baby, we can work this out."

"There's nothing to resolve, my child is dead!"

"It was an accident."

"I shouldn't have been driving. I was…" She bit her lip as tears streamed down her face.

"You were what?" This was the first time she had actually said something about that night.

"I knew you were with her. I went looking for you. I'd had enough." She ran her fingers through her hair.

He stared at her in horror.

"I wasn't careful. I should have just left you. Instead I drove like a maniac and killed my baby." Tears ran down her face as she stared directly at him now. "How do I come to terms with that? How can I?"

Joseph stood frozen to the spot. He had never suspected that she knew before, and it hurt him to see the truth of his mistake play itself over and over again. The affair had been the biggest mistake of his life, and only now did he realize that it had probably cost him his wife; most definitely, it had cost them their child. "We can fix—"

"There's nothing to fix. It can't be fixed. I don't love you. I don't want to hurt anymore. I need some peace. I want to close my eyes and not dream anymore. I want a new life…"

"Without me…" he finished for her.

"Yes."

She left the room, leaving him staring at the door.

Gabriella walked out into the hallway feeling empty, yet a great relief came over her. It was all out; it had finally been voiced. Gabriella knew where she wanted to go. How would Blayne react to her coming to her? She opted to take a chance; she was through running. The only time she felt peace these days was in Blayne's arms.

Chapter Thirteen

Gabriella walked into Blayne's room without knocking. The truth was she didn't want to take the chance of being turned away. She was surprised to find the room empty. Gabriella sat on the bed for a while, then got up and walked around the room. She noticed things she had not seen before. The photos on a nearby bureau were the first to catch her eye.

Gabriella walked closer and noticed how neat and orderly it all was. They were prize photos. Blayne looked very serious and a little too stiff, she thought. They were all pictures of some award being presented or another. She looked around the room and noticed the austereness of all that surrounded her. This was a place she slept in; it wasn't home. What had Blayne said to her? This was a place she stayed in, but home was her house by the sea.

Gabriella lay down and closed her eyes, trying to imagine what home to Blayne was as she drifted off to sleep.

A few hours later, a loud bang woke her up. She sat up, rubbing her eyes, and came face to face with a very angry woman staring at her from the door.

"Get out!" Blayne spat at Gabriella as she walked into the bathroom.

A few minutes later, Blayne walked out with a robe on and stopped abruptly when she saw that Gabriella was still there. "I'm too tired to fuck you. Get out, Gabriella."

"Blayne…" Her eyes pleaded for understanding.

"Don't you have any shame?" Blayne asked in disgust.

"No, not where you're concerned. I love you," Gabriella said as she got up.

"You don't know what love is. Go take care of your daughter, who's miserable, and leave me alone."

"What about Elle?" Gabriella asked, the concern obvious in her face.

"She's scared to death of high school. She's only thirteen. Why are you pushing her so hard?"

"I didn't realize…I thought…" Gabriella seemed to drift off in thought.

"You thought? Try asking her once in a while," Blayne said angrily. "You have no clue how frightening the world is to her right now."

Gabriella looked into her eyes in distress. She realized that she had been so wrapped up in her own life that she had not seen just how unhappy Elle was. Her eyes filled with tears as she realized how much she had failed her daughter.

Blayne told herself she was not going to get pulled in by those eyes again.

Blayne walked toward the door and opened it. "Get out."

"I don't want to go. Please, come here."

Blayne slammed the door and was in front of her almost as if she had flown. She grabbed Gabriella by the hair and pulled her head back as she roughly pulled her body toward her. "Is this what you want?"

Gabriella tried pulling away.

"Oh, no, you don't." Blayne pulled her head toward her and took her mouth. "This is what you deserve."

Gabriella noticed the smell of liquor on her breath. "Stop it, you're drunk."

Blayne then pushed her away so hard that Gabriella

slammed into the wall and stared in fear at Blayne.

"Yes, I'm drunk. I'm drunk on my own blood. It's the only way I can stand you!"

"You don't mean that."

"Don't I? You opened my eyes, little sister. I have found that I like a lot of things." She smiled wickedly. "With you, I began my education…" She walked toward Gabriella again. "Shall I show you what I learned tonight?"

Gabriella stared in confusion. "What you learned tonight?"

"Did you think I would wait for you forever?" Blayne taunted her.

Gabriella suddenly understood, and the shock showed. "No," she uttered as she shook her head. She didn't want to know; she didn't want to hear that someone else had touched Blayne's body, kissed her, made love to her. The mere thought of it was cutting her to pieces.

Blayne smiled and nodded. She was glad that Gabriella was hurting. Why shouldn't she hurt? "Smell me…can you smell another woman on me, little sister? Can you imagine where she touched me, how I fucked her?"

"No!" Gabriella threw herself at Blayne and was caught in a tight embrace as she tried to strike her over and over again.

"I'm going to give you what you came for." Blayne growled and kissed her hard until she began to taste blood in her mouth. Blayne's hands were rough and demanding.

"I love you. I love you." Gabriella wept, and as much as she had fought Blayne before, now she clung to her as her body shook with her weeping. "Oh, god, I love you."

Blayne pulled at her clothes, trying to stay angry. She didn't want to love Gabriella; loving her hurt more than breathing. She was dying; the fever that needing Gabriella produced in her was killing her. She didn't want to hear the sobbing of the woman she loved.

"I love you…" Gabriella's voice broke her heart.

Finally, Blayne pulled Gabriella to her in a tight embrace as they both fell to the floor against the bed and she held her fiercely as her own tears began. Blayne couldn't—she didn't want to—fight her need for Gabriella any longer.

Gabriella looked up and met the eyes that had captivated her and taken her prisoner from the very first moment in what seemed like a lifetime ago. Blayne was about to speak when Gabriella kissed her before she could. Gabriella kissed her wantonly as her tears continued. She wept as she made love to Blayne. Her tears were of sadness, need, joy, passion, and the inevitability of knowing that no matter what, Blayne was something she needed to survive.

They made love slowly, and between tears and caresses, they reached something within that had not been touched before. Their passionate surrender ultimately had been gentle and most of all, a giving of the self to each other. The pain had blown the doors that had been shut long ago wide open. They were both exposed, both needing and clinging to each other.

They lay on the bed much later holding each other without speaking. Blayne almost felt the moment Gabriella began to weep anew; she pulled the woman she loved tighter to her as she whispered in her ear, "I didn't sleep with her."

"Thank god." Gabriella let out a loud sob that spoke of the pain her soul had been feeling as she buried her face in Blayne's neck. Her body shook with the crying. She kissed Blayne's face and neck as she clung to her in desperation. Gabriella had never imagined that something could hurt as much as when she thought Blayne had given herself to another. "Thank god." Gabriella kissed her lightly on the lips.

Blayne tasted Gabriella's tears on her mouth, and her

eyes hid nothing from the woman in her arms as she spoke.

"How could I? You are embedded so deeply inside me that no one will ever do. Don't you know that? What I feel for you is stronger than love." Blayne kissed Gabriella's hair as she tightened her hold.

"Blayne! Blayne!"

Blayne sat up in shock as the door burst open. She stared at her mother who seemed to have frozen in front of them. Gabriella sat up, as well, and grabbed for the sheet to cover herself as she turned her face away from Abigail.

The whole world seemed to collapse around them as Joseph entered the room, as well.

"Gabriella?" he uttered in disbelief, taking in the horrific scene in front of him.

Gabriella lay on her side, covering her face as she began to shake.

Blayne suddenly came to life.

"Get out! Everyone, get out!" She got up uncaring as her mother covered her mouth at her nakedness and Joseph seemed to get madder. "Now!"

"Gabriella!" Joseph walked deeper into the room.

Gabriella then sat up, covering her breasts with the sheet that had become her shield. "Please go, I…"

"This is what you…" Joseph just stared, and he looked from Gabriella to Blayne.

Blayne opened a closet and pulled out a while silk robe and put it on without looking in her mother's direction. Abigail had not yet said a word.

"This is not the place to talk." Blayne tried to control the situation.

"Mom…Mom?" Elle and Christopher walked in and stared at the adults.

"Oh, god, no, no." Gabriella cried.

"Please, Joseph. Not now, please," Blayne said gently, looking from him to the children.

He stared at her with a murderous gleam in his eyes, then spat at Gabriella as he grabbed the children and dragged them with him.

Gabriella covered her face and sobbed as she fell back on the bed.

"Blayne..." Abigail said softly.

Blayne turned toward her mother and was about to speak when Abigail pre-empted her.

"Your father is dead."

It had all happened so quickly in the beginning. Somehow they had all walked like zombies each in his or her own world for the next few days. Arthur had been buried two days later. His funeral had received much press coverage, and it was noted that the line of cars of the cemetery procession was the longest that Quincy had ever had for one of her sons.

Blayne, as expected, had taken care of the arrangements, and the only thing that was seen was a united front. They all stood side by side along the grave as Arthur was lowered into the ground. Chaz was holding up Abigail as she openly wept. Blayne looked toward Gabriella. Their gazes locked emotionless for a mere second but enough to convey what was to come.

The gathering after the funeral was held at the estate with as much pomp and circumstance as people of their social status required and expected. Not once did Gabriella and Blayne speak.

The day after the burial, Joseph and his family packed up their suitcases, and a limousine took them to the airport.

Diana had taken a distraught Abigail to her room as Blayne was seeing off a few family members who had stayed at the estate for the funeral.

Chaz stayed out of the way and waited in the wings. Now the tide must be ridden out carefully, he told himself. The will would be read in a few weeks, and for now, Blayne was still at its head.

Chapter Fourteen

"Blayne?" Diana walked out onto the balcony and up to her sister. Blayne had not seemed to have heard her.

Diana stared at the back of her sister sadly. Perhaps she, more than anyone, knew just how much this must hurt.

"Yes, Diana…" Blayne said without turning.

"I thought you hadn't heard me." Diana leaned on the balcony in front of her.

Blayne said nothing and continued to stare into the night.

"Mother is resting finally. I'm sorry I wasn't more help with the rest of the guests."

"It's all right, it's all finished now," Blayne said.

"Blayne, why did she go?"

Blayne turned toward Diana and what Diana saw in her eyes broke her heart.

Blayne walked back into the house without uttering a word.

Diana stared at her sadly as she watched her leave.

"Leila?"

Gabriella turned and smiled as her mother walked into her studio.

"Hello, Mama. What brings you by?" she said without getting up from the stool she sat on while she worked on a block of plaster.

"I just wanted to make sure you were all right."

"I'm fine."

"Are you?" Her mother pulled up another stool and sat next to her daughter as she stared at the piece that Gabriella had been working on.

"Yes."

"Are you still angry with me?" Elena asked as she looked shamefully at Gabriella.

"No..." Gabriella put down the carving tool and took her mother's hands into her own. "I was never angry with you, Mama."

"Then why all this?"

"What?"

"It's been weeks and you'

re not here. You didn't come back," Elena said desperately.

"Mama, what are you talking about?"

"You haven't been the same."

"Time changes us all, Mama," Gabriella said sadly but smiled.

"It's more than that. I even see it in your work." Her mother looked around the studio as she spoke. "There is a sadness that permeates it all."

Gabriella looked away. "No, it's all okay. I've just been tired, that's all."

"How are things with Joseph?"

"Fine, things are fine." Gabriella picked up the scalpel again.

"Why don't you leave him?"

Gabriella turned to face her mother again, and the shock on her face showed. "Why would you say something like that?"

"Because you're walking around like the dead. I want to see my daughter. If being here with him means this...we never wanted that for you. I know that Papa and I used to… but not like this." Elena's eyes filled with tears. "We wanted you to be happy. He's a good provider. I wanted you…"

"Mama…" Gabriella took her mother into her arms. "I stayed with Joseph because I wanted to. No one made me do anything."

"All I have ever wanted for you is to have a good life. I wanted you to be happy, to know love."

"I know love, Mama, I know love," Gabriella said sadly.

Elena pulled away from the embrace and stared deeply into her daughter's eyes.

"It's not Joseph, is it?" It had been a question, but her mother knew as soon as her daughter's eyes became sadder.

"Of course it is." Gabriella looked away too quickly.

"You fell in love," Elena said simply.

"Mama, don't do this…" Gabriella walked away and wrapped her arms around herself.

"Leila…"

"No! I can't do this with you. I'm not strong enough for this," Gabriella said desperately. "Please…leave me alone."

Elena stared at Gabriella and saw the pain in her features. She knew the signs all too well, and it cut her deeply that her child should feel the same pain that had marked her whole life.

"Does he love you?"

Gabriella closed her eyes as tears ran down her face. Her body began to shake as the sobbing got louder.

Elena was next to her immediately and embraced her. "Oh, *mi nina. No llores, mi nina.*" Elena asked her child not to cry as she cried herself.

She had always prayed that her daughter would find love. When Gabriella had brought Joseph home, she could tell her choice was to please her father. He had wanted her to have a secure future and Gabriella adored him. She had at the time thought that perhaps it would be best. And as the years passed by, she saw the change come over Gabriella so slowly. Gabriella was only herself when she was working or with the children.

Elena now realized that love was beating strongly within her daughter's heart. She knew her child. She also knew the signs. And what she saw broke her heart.

"Who is he?" Elena asked.

Gabriella then pulled away. "I can't do this, Mama, I can't."

"Does he love you?"

"Please…" Gabriella begged.

"Let me help you."

"You can't help me. No one can help me," Gabriella said in frustration. "No one would understand!"

"Leila, I don't care if you want to start a new life with this man. I'll help you. And what does it matter if people don't understand?"

"It's not that simple…" Gabriella sat down and looked away.

"I know it's not. People divorce now. The children love you. I love you. Joseph in time will have to accept this. I'll help you, Leila." Her mother placed her hands over her daughter's.

"Would you?" Gabriella said as she looked up with tear-filled eyes. "I don't think so."

Elena looked taken aback. "Why would you say that?"

Gabriella stared at her mother, wanting to believe that the words were true, but she knew it could never be.

"Elena," Joseph said from the door with a smile. "What a nice surprise. Can you stay for dinner?"

Both women turned as Joseph walked into the studio. Gabriella turned back to her sculpture.

"Hello, Joseph," Elena said politely.

He walked up to Gabriella and kissed her lightly on the cheek. "How is the piece coming along, sweetheart?"

"Making good progress today."

"Good, good."

Elena looked at her daughter, then at Joseph. She had sat by her whole life and just let others dictate what she should do. Gabriella had to have a choice. She would see that she did.

"Joseph, can you leave us for a few minutes? I need to speak with my daughter."

Joseph looked at her surprised and nodded as he left them.

Elena watched as he walked out of the studio and closed the door behind him. She then turned to her daughter and took a deep breath. Gabriella's back was still to her.

"He's a good man. But he's not for you," Elena said flatly.

Gabriella closed her eyes tight and wished she could just not hear another word.

"Tell me why you're sitting there and not fighting for what you want. Do you want to end up like me?"

Gabriella faced her.

"Yes, you heard me." Elena was angry. "Your father was a good man, too. But I didn't love him. I'm sorry you have to hear that, but it's true." Elena's eyes were spilling over with tears, too. "I was in love with another man. I always had been."

Gabriella wept openly as she saw the pain in her mother materialize. She had always known that there was this great sadness, but she had never understood why.

"I don't want this for you." Elena cried. "Because you are like me. It will be with you your whole life."

"Mama…please, don't."

"I have to. I won't let this happen to you, too."

"You don't understand."

"Then make me understand!" Elena cried out in desperation.

"I'm in love with a woman!" Gabriella yelled in frustration. When she saw the shock in her mother's face, she turned around. She could not face it.

They were surrounded with silence in what seemed like a lifetime. Then finally, Gabriella spoke.

"It just happened. I look at her and I…" Gabriella said sadly. "No one would understand. Not even you."

"Who is she?" Elena asked soberly. "Do I know her?"

"You met her briefly."

"Blayne Anberville," Elena said.

Gabriella turned again and saw the expression of disbelief on her mother's face.

"Do you see now, Mama?"

Elena stared back at her daughter. "Did she seduce you?"

"No…I wanted her as much as she wanted me," Gabriella said honestly. "I'm the one that left her. She loved me and I simply walked away from her," Gabriella finished as tears ran down her face.

Elena looked at her child, walked up to her, and took her once again in her arms.

"Mama, it hurts so much. It hurts so much." Gabriella wept as her mother's arms tightened around her.

"Chaz, where's your sister?" Abigail asked her son as she walked to the garden.

"She's around here somewhere. Are you feeling better, Mother?"

Abigail had been inconsolable for the last few weeks, but that particular morning, she got up and wanted to settle some things in her home.

"I am, thank you," Abigail said as her eyes misted over. "I miss him."

"I know. We all do." Chaz looked away. He had loved Arthur in his own way. He had to admit that the old man had never tired of trying to "make something out of him," as he used to put it.

"Chaz, we'll all need each other now. I don't want to lose any of you."

Chaz looked at her. "Mother…"

"You three are all I have. And you three are all you have."

Chaz stared at her not understanding.

"As much as you fight it, Blayne and Diana will always be a part of you. They carry your blood, and in the end, they are all you will be able to count on. Remember that, my son. Always remember that." Abigail walked away, leaving him to analyze the words.

"Where is she, Diana?"

Diana smiled at her mother.

"Where's your sister?"

"Is everything all right, Mother?"

"It will be once I take care of a few things," Abigail said angrily.

"Mother…"

"Where is she?"

"Blayne is by the pond."

Abigail then left her as she went looking for Blayne.

"Mother, she's had a rough time lately…" Diana said with concern.

Abigail looked back and nodded in acknowledgment before she began walking again.

"We've all had a rough time lately," Abigail mumbled

to herself. She was going to deal with Blayne and the circumstances in which she had found her in with Gabriella. It was time to get things back on track. They had to or they would all fall apart. She felt the aura of death all around her and she feared it.

It had been four weeks since Arthur died. And the pain of losing him was still raw inside Blayne. He had always seen the best in her, and it hurt to know that she would never be able to make him understand her nor could she erase the look of disapproval in his face from her mind. She had grown thin from missing meals and she felt listless and empty.

Blayne was also ignoring the business. She just didn't care anymore. Gabriella was gone and she would forever want her. Blayne knew that as surely as she knew her life would never again hold any beauty. She carried her sadness deep within her. Only when she was alone like this did she allow it to surface and take what little relief weeping gifted her with.

Blayne sat and leaned her back against the tree as she faced the pond. Arthur and she had come here so often when she was a child. God, how she missed him, and she thought of how much of a disappointment she had been to him in the end.

She could almost make herself feel Gabriella lightly kiss her lips as the wind blew by. A deep sob rose from within her filled with so much sorrow that she thought she would die at that instant. Blayne sobbed without covering her face as she looked toward the sky.

Abigail froze and stared in horror. She had never thought to see her child in such pain. All the anger inside her disappeared as she faced the incredible sorrow of the scene before her.

She had received a concerned call from Harry Bancroft earlier that morning. He was worried that business matters were being overlooked and that Blayne had been virtually unreachable for weeks. None of that mattered now as Abigail stared in shock. She watched as Blayne cried without consolation. She wept like something wounded and dying. The strong woman that Abigail knew as her daughter was simply not there. Before her was a young woman who cried as if her heart was ripped from her.

"Why didn't you kill me?" Blayne pleaded between the crying. "Why did you leave me to this, Gabriella?" The tears ran down her face unchecked. "I love you."

The last words broke Abigail's heart as she heard them. She walked away, leaving her daughter holding the pieces of a broken heart.

As she walked back to the house, she thought many things. And then she took a deep breath and resolved to change what she could. This was Arthur's legacy. And it occurred to her that she didn't want it to be hers.

Abigail didn't speak to Blayne that day nor did she ever broach the subject of Gabriella. The will had been read, and it held no surprises. Arthur, as it turned out, never changed it, and all was left mostly to Abigail with the exception of a few things to trusted and faithful employees. It had, however, been clearly stipulated that Blayne would always have the majority voting shares in the company. So in effect, Blayne had been left with control.

Diana shrugged it off, and Chaz somehow seemed to accept it. He had packed up and was touring the Riviera again for the winter. Diana had stayed close to home and close to Blayne. Abigail just watched and waited. In time, she had to believe that Blayne would become her old self again.

And as the weeks became months, the semblance of the old Blayne became evident and Abigail breathed a sigh of relief. Her family had managed to survive it all. It was as if Gabriella and her mother had never existed.

With this, Abigail began to breathe easier. She was preparing for the holidays and was expecting her children to arrive momentarily.

Diana got home first. "Hello, Mother." She walked up and kissed her mother's cheek.

"Hello, darling," Abigail said as she put another fixture on the tree.

"Chaz arrive from Monte Carlo yet?"

"Last night," Abigail said with a smile.

"And Blayne?"

"She's running late but will be here after dinner." Abigail continued to decorate the tree.

"I haven't seen her for a while. Have you spoken with her recently?" Diana sat close to where her mother was.

"You know how Blayne is. She's very busy these days and doesn't have time to call that often."

Diana frowned at the flippant way her mother was taking things. The last time she had seen Blayne was like seeing and speaking to a stranger.

"Well, I guess we shall see how she is when she gets here tonight."

Blayne never made it for the decorating that evening; she called to say she was tied up at the office. She promised to come but could not give a time as to when. She asked them to go to bed and she would eventually arrive and they would spend Christmas Day together.

Blayne walked into a silent house. She passed by the great room and saw the decorated tree. She stood in front of it for a moment and realized that it looked the same way year after year. Except that this would be the first year without her father. She smiled sadly at how Arthur loved giving out presents in the morning. And as always, good memories were followed by the ones that haunted her every time she closed her eyes. At least during the day, she could fill her hours with work, but the nights would inevitably bring the same dreams over and over again.

She walked quietly toward the library. It occurred to her that this was her favorite room in this house. So much living had been done here. Here she'd had long talks with her father and here in the same room she had loved and held Gabriella. And as she felt the power that merely remembering held over her, she closed her eyes, trying to shut out living. Because living was just too painful and just existing was easier.

She had intentionally not come earlier. She wasn't exactly sure how she would react with everyone. It had been months since she'd come to visit. The house, the grounds, everything looked the same. Even the Christmas tree held the old and comfortable visage. But life was not as she wished it was. If granted one wish, what would she wish for? What did she want for Christmas?

It was easy. She would wish to live one hour over and over again for the rest of her life. She walked toward the window and stared out. How many times had she stood in the same spot throughout the years searching and not finding the answers of what she wanted for herself? Sadly, now she knew. The one thing she wanted she would never have.

She looked down and saw the burgundy decanter and poured herself a large drink. Looking at it for a moment, she then raised it to her lips. Before drinking, she raised it up and celebrated her anguish. "Merry Christmas, my darling." As the tears ran down her face, she drank all the contents within the glass.

Blayne poured the amber liquid into the glass once more

and filled it to the rim. She then took the glass with her as she headed up the stairs toward her bedroom.

She never noticed the dark figure that had remained silent in the room.

Elena hurried to open the door to stop the persistent knocking. In front of her stood an elegant woman.

"Can I help you?" Elena asked politely.

"Yes, I hope you can. My name is Abigail Aston-Carlyle."

Chapter Fifteen

Elena stood surprised. Both women searched the other's face for some kind of sign. In the end, they realized there was nothing but a past between them.

"May I come in?" Abigail asked.

"Yes, please." Elena stepped to the side and let Abigail in.

Abigail walked into the small but cozy living room. She saw the photographs of a lifetime on the walls and coffee table.

Elena watched as Arthur's widow inspected the photographs that comprised her life.

Abigail stopped in front of a photograph of a young Gabriella on top of a pony. The sun had caught the little girl in such a way that her blue eyes seemed just like those of her father. Abigail picked up the photo and smiled sadly.

"Arthur loved horses…" Abigail could not keep the sadness from her voice.

"Yes…"

Abigail closed her eyes at those words as she turned to look at the woman who had always been between her and the man she loved.

"Won't you sit down?" Elena said as she pointed to the nearby sofa.

"Yes, thank you." She put down Gabriella's photograph, walked over to the sofa, and sat.

"Can I offer you something to drink?"

"No, thank you," Abigail said as she looked down at the floor and Elena sat in an armchair in front of her. "He never stopped loving you," Abigail said to a surprised Elena. "Even in the end. His last words were for you." Tears ran down Abigail's face as she saw the pain register on Elena's face.

"I…" Elena looked away. She didn't want to know. What good would it do?

"He woke up clutching his chest with your name on his lips."

Elena turned toward the woman in front of her now and shared her pain.

"He died saying your name."

"I'm sorry" was all that Elena managed to say.

Abigail then got up and walked to the bow window and stared out to the street. "I'm here because this has to end."

"I don't understand," Elena said in confusion.

"I think you do. I don't want this for my daughter. And I don't think you want this for yours," Abigail said bluntly and turned to face Elena. As soon as she saw Elena's face, she knew she had been right.

"I don't know what you're talking about," Elena said, trying to hide her growing nervousness.

"Blayne is an exceptional woman. She's one of those people that are good and fine. And she is slowly dying of love. I have stood by all these months…I won't any longer."

"I don't understand," Elena said in agitation.

"Don't you?" Abigail faced her. "I found them together. Is that blunt enough for you?"

"I don't want to hear this." Elena got up quickly. "Please leave my house."

"I know this is difficult. I've been trying to forget it and just ignore it, but the reality is that my daughter is in a great deal of pain, and I know that yours must be, too." Abigail appealed to the woman in front of her whose semblance looked stern and unyielding.

"Gabriella is just fine. I'm sorry," Elena said as she was walking toward the front door to let Abigail out.

"I don't want my daughter to be a homosexual." The words stopped Elena and made her turn around. She saddened as she saw her own pain mirrored in Abigail's eyes. "I don't want that kind of life for her."

Elena remained quiet as she looked away.

"Blayne has always been a tower of strength. She's strong and proud. She's all those clichés that used to apply in my day. My daughter is the best of us all. Even Arthur couldn't change that."

Elena stared at her in confusion now.

Abigail took a deep breath. "He loved the children in his own way. He wanted to shape them in his vision. Chaz simply rebelled, coming up short all the time, and decided to do nothing with his life. Diana is pretty much the same. She wanders aimlessly and doesn't even try. Blayne was the one that excelled in everything and had all his attention. He doted on her and she adored him. Blayne was everything he wanted except for one thing."

Elena waited patiently. It saddened her that Arthur was indeed a man who had not deserved to be loved by so many.

"Blayne wouldn't marry. She couldn't seem to find someone and give him the grandchildren he wanted to leave his legacy to. They would argue endlessly, but she would never give in. And of course, a part of him was proud that she was so strong," Abigail finished sadly.

"He was generous with Elle and Christopher," Elena said as she sat again.

"Arthur never changed his will," Abigail said bluntly.

Elena looked up at her in confusion.

"Not even at the end did he stop being the selfish egocentric man that he was. I loved him, but that's the truth."

"But the trust funds for Elle and Christopher…"

"I was there when they read the will. If the trust funds came from anyone, it was Blayne. He left her control of everything." Abigail sat down, as well, looking weary. "Blayne is drinking, which is not like her. My daughter carries this incredible sadness that's really frightening me." Abigail looked up at Elena with tear-filled eyes.

Elena looked away. She didn't want to hear this, and a part of her resented her daughter for this manifestation.

"If anything happens to her, Gabriella will never know another day's peace."

"Is that a threat?" Elena said angrily as she turned toward Abigail.

"No…" Abigail continued sadly. "I saw them…I saw as they reached out to each other. I should have seen it for what it was right from the beginning. They have this understanding between them. I know that Arthur found out and demanded that Blayne stay away. That has also hurt her so much. She lost her father and lost the only person she'll ever love the same day."

"In time…it may pass, you don't know that it won't…" Elena began to say.

"If anything happens to Blayne, Gabriella will never forgive herself. I saw them together…that's how I know."

Elena got up and wrapped her arms around herself; she wasn't sure what to do or what to think. Would her Leila truly feel that way? Could she see beyond her prejudices and accept this? She just wasn't sure she could.

"At Christmas, my daughter was barely the woman I knew. At that time, she was at least in the world of the living.

It's the first Christmas Eve she was not there for. Her brother actually waited for her. He came up to my room that night… I have never seen Chaz worry about her. That night, he was. Blayne has always been their anchor…" Abigail gasped for air as the tears overwhelmed her again. "She has since then avoided us all."

Abigail sat and took out a handkerchief from her purse and wiped her tears. "Two months ago, she just stopped going into the office and flew to her house in Cape Cod. I was angry, we are all so angry and confused. I had this premonition, and I went to see her a few days ago. What I found has brought me here to you…" Abigail cried in earnest and her body shook.

Elena immediately went to her and sat next to her.

"I found a stranger. Thin and gaunt, I don't think she even knew I was there. She just stares out into the ocean. I'm frightened."

Elena got up. "I'm sorry."

Abigail got up, too, disappointed that she had not been able to touch Elena's heart. "Arthur's legacy has been one of pain and sorrow. We don't have to let it continue," Abigail pleaded.

Elena walked toward the door, and this time, Abigail followed. Before she was out of the house, she handed Elena a card.

"We can still change things. I think you love your Gabriella very much. Is she happy? Look at her, really look at her, then call me. It's too late for you and me, not for them. They can still have their happiness."

Elena took the card and stood at her door until the limousine disappeared around the corner.

Gabriella stared at the piece of marble in front of her and could not concentrate. The peace that she received from her work had slowly but surely been less present each day. She closed her eyes and leaned her forehead against the cool stone, and as always, visions of a beautiful face flooded her mind.

"Blayne…" she said softly. "Where are you? I feel you so close today. Are you thinking of me? Blayne…" Her eyes remained closed as she cried.

Elle had been standing by the door with her grandmother and heard her mother's words. They all thought she was just a kid, but a lot of things made sense to her now. She saw the tears on her mother's face. She walked up to her, and Gabriella took her into her arms and wept.

"Don't cry, Mommy. Don't cry, it's going to be okay." Elle caressed her mother's hair, trying to comfort her; Elena stood quietly by the doorframe. Gabriella had not noticed them until Elle went up to her.

"I know, baby. Mommy is just a little sad today. I'm fine, don't you worry, okay?" Gabriella held on to her child. Her children made it bearable. Her need for Blayne seemed to be encompassing every aspect of her life to the point that she felt as if she could hardly breathe.

"Abuela is here," Elle said, looking toward her grandmother.

Gabriella wiped her face clean before turning toward her mother. "Hola, Mama." She smiled as she got up and went to kiss her mother on the cheek. "Can you stay for lunch?"

"That would be nice."

"Thank you for coming, Blayne," Neil said as he walked up to her. "She refused to speak to anyone else but you."

Neil Tedesco was one of her most competent VPs, and he had called her and had continued to call her until she finally agreed to come.

"Yes, apparently," Blayne said cynically as she walked

around the desk and sat. "What's the problem?"

"Everything went smoothly until it came time to sign the contracts. She insists on meeting with you first. Nothing would deter her. I'm sorry. I know you didn't want to be disturbed, but there was no other way. I've tried everything," Neil finished in exasperation.

She waved her hand as if tired of the whole thing. "Fine, when will she be here?"

"She's here now. Do you want me to bring her here or would you rather we meet in the boardroom?"

"Here...bring her here." Blayne leaned back into the chair and closed her eyes.

Neil seemed unsure and didn't move. He could tell Blayne had lost weight and seemed rather pale. What had happened to the once energetic and powerful presence he knew as Blayne Anberville? One day almost six months before, she had just not shown up. Seeing her now, he realized that something was very wrong. The woman seemed frail and vulnerable. The vitality that she always exuded was not present in her.

When Blayne finally noticed that he had not moved from where he stood, she opened her eyes and stared at him. "Well? Go get her. I don't have all day."

He seemed to spring into action at that moment and left her. She was irritable, she knew that. She didn't want to be here. Responsibility, accountability, respectability were words that made up who she was for so long. Blayne wasn't sure why she had come. The company could almost run itself, she knew that. Besides, she had...they all had enough money to live many lifetimes over. What did it matter if one deal was lost or two or three? She just didn't care anymore. All she wanted was to be alone with her memories and her disgust of what she had allowed herself to become.

That morning when Neil called had been harsher than

the ones before. There seemed to be so many...so many mornings, nights, and days now; as the specter of them spread before her, the ocean had become too inviting. It had frightened her. It wasn't so much that she feared dying or the thought that finally her need and loneliness would end, but the thought that she had actually wanted it so badly had shaken her. Neil's call was like a horn calling her into shore...throwing her a lifeline if she only wanted to reach out and take it.

Now as she sat in her old chair, she looked around at the things that once meant the world to her. Her triumphs were all framed on the walls. And just as her head dropped forward at the sadness that suddenly filled her soul, the door opened.

Blayne had not heard the door open or close. She raised her head with her eyes closed and leaned it back again. This was a mistake, she told herself. When the meeting was over, she would go back to the Cape. It had finally all sunk in... her past, even its bits and pieces, was unbearable to her.

"I'm sorry. I didn't know you were ill." A soft voice brought her head forward, and her eyes opened quickly.

Blayne stared at the woman in front of her in cold disdain. "Please sit down." Her lips turned up into a polite smile, but the message her eyes were conveying was harshly cruel.

"Truly, Blayne, I'm sorry."

Blayne nodded and waited. When Tara Montgomery said nothing, she got up and walked toward the large picture window and stared out onto the city of Boston. "How high up we are. From up here, the world seems so small."

Tara watched her in fascination. "Why have you been avoiding this meeting?"

Blayne smiled sadly, still looking out. "I wasn't avoiding you, Tara. I don't want to be here."

Tara stood and walked toward her. "This whole deal was

put together because of you."

"I know."

"Pretty cocky, aren't you?" Tara said playfully.

"No, just tired of playing games." Blayne turned to her.

They both looked at each other without saying a word.

"I don't want to play, Tara. I told you that night at the club in Quincy." Blayne broke eye contact first as she ran her fingers through her hair. "This is a good deal. If you want it, sign the contracts. If you don't, don't."

"Is she so deep inside you that you've stopped walking with the living?" Tara said venomously. "Jesus, look at you. You look like shit!"

Blayne remained silent.

"My god...you love her that much?" Tara asked incredulously.

"Ms. Montgomery, my personal life is neither here nor there. As I recall, you and I shared a dance and a kiss in a dark club in Quincy, and that's all," Blayne said irately. "Having said that, will you sign these contracts or not?"

"I want you. I want to get to know you. I want you to get to know me. I wouldn't hurt you."

Blayne looked away as Tara's eyes filled with tears. "You are quite right, Ms. Montgomery. I barely know you and you barely know me. I'm not worth knowing, I assure you."

"I know more than you can imagine. I just got to your life late." Tara took a step closer. "I fell in love with you the moment I saw you at the Copley."

Blayne smiled and laughed. "What are you talking about? We didn't meet at the Copley. You have one of the protagonists in this imaginary love affair mistaken for someone else."

"I had come to Boston to meet with you. I was staying at the Copley. When there you were...Blayne Anberville... bigger than life standing next to me in the elevator. I recognized you from a photograph I once saw in *Fortune*. I wanted you right then. I was going to speak to you in the elevator when I saw a tear roll down your cheek."

Blayne's eyes searched her face and saw the truth of her words. She remembered, as well.

"That's the moment it happened. As you walked out of the elevator, I felt the loss of you and I knew. I'm in love with you, Blayne. No games, this is my truth," Tara finished as tears ran down her face. "I know you can love me…I know I can make you happy. I would at least ask for a chance to try."

"Tara…" Blayne looked down, not finding the words.

"I can make you forget her," Tara said miserably.

Blayne looked up sadly. "No one can take her place. She's in all I am. I'm sorry." Blayne began to walk away.

"Please, give me a chance." Tara grabbed her arm and turned her around. "Just one chance."

"Goodbye, Tara." Blayne walked out, leaving her standing in the middle of the office.

As soon as Blayne left, Neil walked in the office not sure what he would be met with.

"Ms. Montgomery?" he said tentatively as he approached. "Is everything all right?"

Tara wiped her face and turned around with a bright smile. "Yes, all is fine, Mr. Tedesco. Where are those contracts?"

"Here they are." Neil smiled and walked up to the desk and handed her a pen to sign the papers.

"Thank you." Tara smiled sweetly.

Tara signed all four copies, then stood straight. "Well, it seems that our business is concluded then."

"Thank you. I'll have copies sent to your attorneys." Neil shook her hand and smiled to himself as he saw her walking away.

As soon as Tara Montgomery turned away from him, her

smile faded and sadness once again filled her eyes. Every step she took was a painful one. She knew that each step was farther and farther from love. "I was late, my love. I was late."

Chapter Sixteen

Gabriella walked up to Joseph and stood next to him. They looked out onto the garden—both silent, both waiting.

"Joseph…" Gabriella began after a few minutes.

"I know," he said as his head leaned down.

"I'm sorry."

He nodded.

"The kids…"

"The kids are going to be fine." He straightened up, staring out into the garden again. "They're like you. They're strong."

"I wanted it to be forever," Gabriella said as she cried.

"I know." They both stood silently. "Are you going to her?"

"No."

Joseph turned toward her in surprise.

"There's just too large of an ocean between us. Mama…" Gabriella trailed off as she looked down.

"Elena knows?"

"I told her."

"We could try, Gabriella," Joseph said hopefully.

"I can't do this anymore. I'm sorry. I know I'm hurting you."

"I'll move out tonight." He left her standing on the deck.

Gabriella let the tears fall. A part of her life was over.

Diana had been home for a few weeks and had managed to keep her mother occupied and busy. She tried getting in touch with Blayne, but her calls were never taken.

"Mother, Jack called and he has an extra ticket to the symphony. Why not come with us?"

"No, dear, you go. I'm just going to retire early."

"Mother…I'm worried about you," Diana said tenderly as she walked up to Abigail.

"I'm concerned about Blayne. I went to see her a few days ago. She looks awful. She's wasting away, and I can't stop it."

"Mother…"

The ringing of the telephone interrupted their conversation. Abigail picked up the receiver.

"Hello?"

Her face showed surprise as she listened, and surprise gradually turned into a smile.

"Leila."

Gabriella turned slowly, then smiled as she walked up to her mother. "Mama, I didn't know you were here."

"I came to speak to my grandchildren."

Gabriella looked at her curiously.

"I especially spoke with Elle. She's an incredible young woman."

Gabriella smiled. "She's growing up so fast, Mama. Sometimes I wish I could keep her my little girl forever."

"I know. But if you love them, Leila, you must let them go."

Gabriella now searched her mother's face. Elena took her daughter's hand and walked her to the small sofa on the side of the studio that faced the garden. When they were seated, Elena took her daughter's hands into her own and held them.

"Parents want only the best for their children."

"Yes, Mama."

"Sometimes, our best wishes aren't what they want for themselves." Elena looked deeply into her child's eyes. "I have always wanted so much for you."

Gabriella smiled.

"When you were born and they put you in my arms, I believed in miracles again, Leila. From that moment on, I promised myself that you would have all the things that I…" Elena looked down, then up again and continued. "I wanted you to love and be loved in return. I wanted you to know the joy of a family and children."

"Mama…" Gabriella's eyes were filling with tears. "I promised you I wouldn't…"

"You promised me that you wouldn't go to her," Elena voiced the unspoken words that had been a barrier between them for so long.

Gabriella remained silent, looking down at her hands being held by her mother's.

Elena smiled as her own eyes filled with tears. "You are more than I deserve. You've always made me so proud." Elena released one of her daughter's hands and caressed her child's wet cheek. "You're so beautiful inside and out. You have so much talent. Your father was so proud of you. He would say, 'My beautiful daughter the artist,' with such pride." Elena then took another deep breath. "You're not like him!"

After Elena said the words, Gabriella looked up and knew exactly what her mother had meant. Gabriella then released a loud sob as she leaned forward and went into her mother's arms.

"You're my daughter. And you're the daughter of Humberto Sotomayor." Elena wept with her daughter as she held her tightly. "Your father loved you so much, Leila." Elena then pulled away from her daughter. She wiped her child's face lovingly. "We both just wanted you to be happy."

Gabriella's tears continued to fall.

"I think it's time I let you go and do that."

Gabriella stared at her not sure exactly what she was trying to tell her. "I don't understand."

"You will, my Leila. You will."

It was only the beginning of October, but the wind coming in from the Atlantic was cold, announcing the weather to come. Blayne stood high on the reef neither caring nor feeling the Arctic chill. The days and nights meant nothing to her anymore.

She slept when her body told her to stop and ate when she felt her body fail her, which seemed often of late. She had simply stopped trying to lie to herself. This is where she wanted it to all stop. On top of the reef, she waited. Waited like she had waited so many other times, closing her eyes and dreaming of what would never be. She leaned her head back and smiled. It was becoming so real. She could hear the voices and feel the joy. Blayne was ready to close her eyes and fly into the air and leap into the world that she had created in her dreams, a world where she was happy. A world where she was loved.

"Gabriella..." she said longingly into the wind.

"I'm here, my darling."

"I can't wait anymore," Blayne answered sadly as she took a step closer to the edge. "I want to be with you."

"Turn around and be with me, my love." Gabriella stood a few feet from Blayne. She suddenly realized the danger, and her heart seemed to stop beating. "I'm real, Blayne, and I love you. Please, my darling, I need you so very much.

Turn around and come to me."

Blayne swayed unsure as she opened her eyes. She turned slowly, and as she took in the vision before her, her eyes filled with unshed tears. "Are you really here? Or are you some nightmare to torment me?"

Gabriella stretched her hand out. "Come to me and let me show you."

Blayne noticed movement coming from the house and saw as her mother and Elena helped the children and Diana take suitcases out of the car.

"I'm here if you want me," Gabriella said.

Blayne looked back at Gabriella, then toward the house. At that moment, Abigail and Elena looked at them and waited.

Blayne then turned to look at Gabriella once more.

"I love you, Blayne Samantha Anberville. I hope you have enough room in this house of yours because it's going to be quite full." Gabriella smiled as tears continued to fall.

"Gabriella?" Blayne realized that it was not a dream. She closed the distance between them and pulled Gabriella into her arms. "Gabriella...Gabriella," she kept repeating as she wept and her body shook with the sobbing.

"Forever and always, my darling. Together, forever and always."

About the author

S. Anne Gardner has lived all over the world and is now permanently living on the East Coast of the United States. She has a love that fills her heart and children who fill her life. She works in the field of finance and is a published author. She enjoys sailing, horseback riding, art, traveling, reading, and writing. Her family, her friends, and her music fill her life in a world that is her own.

Other Titles from
Intaglio Publications
www.intagliopub.com

Accidental Love by B.L. Miller	ISBN: 978-1-933113-11-1	$18.50
An Affair of Love by S. Anne Gardner	ISBN: 978-1-933113-86-9	$16.95
Assignment Sunrise by I Christie	ISBN: 978-1-933113-55-5	$16.95
Away From the Dawn by Kate Sweeney	ISBN: 978-1-933113-81-4	$16.95
Bloodlust by Fran Heckrotte	ISBN: 978-1-933113-50-0	$16.95
Chosen, The by Verda Foster	ISBN: 978-1-933113-25-8	$15.25
Code Blue by KatLyn	ISBN: 978-1-933113-09-8	$16.95
Cost of Commitment, The by Lynn Ames	ISBN: 978-1-933113-02-9	$16.95
Compensation by S. Anne Gardner	ISBN: 978-1-933113-57-9	$16.95
Crystal's Heart by B.L. Miller & Verda Foster	ISBN: 978-1-933113-29-6	$18.50
Deception by Erin O'Reilly	ISBN:978-1-933113-87-6	$16.95
Define Destiny by J.M. Dragon	ISBN: 978-1-933113-56-2	$16.95
Flipside of Desire, The by Lynn Ames	ISBN: 978-1-933113-60-9	$15.95
Gift, The by Verda Foster	ISBN: 978-1-933113-03-6	$15.35
Gift of Time by Robin Alexander	ISBN: 978-1-933113-82-1	$16.95
Gloria's Inn by Robin Alexander	ISBN: 978-1-933113-01-2	$14.95
Graceful Waters by B.L. Miller & Verda Foster	ISBN: 978-1-933113-08-1	$17.25
Halls of Temptation by Katie P. Moore	ISBN: 978-1-933113-42-5	$15.50
Heartsong by Lynn Ames	ISBN: 978-1-933113-74-6	$16.95
Hidden Desires by TJ Vertigo	ISBN: 978-1-933113-83-8	$18.95
Illusionist, The by Fran Heckrotte	ISBN: 978-1-933113-31-9	$16.95
Journey's of Discoveries by Ellis Paris Ramsay	ISBN: 978-1-933113-43-2	$16.95
Josie & Rebecca: The Western Chronicles by Vada Foster & B. L. Miller		
	ISBN: 978-1-933113-38-3	$18.99
Murky Waters by Robin Alexander	ISBN: 978-1-933113-33-3	$15.25
New Beginnings by J M Dragon and Erin O'Reilly		
	ISBN: 978-1-933113-76-0	$16.95
Nice Clean Murder, A by Kate Sweeney	ISBN: 978-1-933113-78-4	$16.95
None So Blind by LJ Maas	ISBN: 978-1-933113-44-9	$16.95
Picking Up the Pace by Kimberly LaFontaine	ISBN: 978-1-933113-41-8	$15.50
Preying on Generosity by Kimberly LaFontaine	ISBN 978-1-933113-79-1	$16.95

Price of Fame, The by Lynn Ames	ISBN: 978-1-933113-04-3	$16.75
Private Dancer by T.J. Vertigo	ISBN: 978-1-933113-58-6	$16.95
Revelations by Erin O'Reilly	ISBN: 978-1-933113-75-3	$16.95
Romance For Life by Lori L Lake (editor) and Tara Young (editor)		
	ISBN: 978-1933113-59-3	$16.95
She Waits by Kate Sweeney	ISBN: 978-1-933113-40-1	$15.95
She's the One by Verda Foster and B.L. Miller	ISBN: 978-1-933113-80-7	$16.95
Southern Hearts by Katie P. Moore	ISBN: 978-1-933113-28-9	$14.95
Storm Surge by KatLyn	ISBN: 978-1-933113-06-7	$16.95
Taking of Eden, The by Robin Alexander	ISBN: 978-1-933113-53-1	$15.95
These Dreams by Verda Foster	ISBN: 978-1-933113-12-8	$15.75
Traffic Stop by Tara Wentz	ISBN: 978-1-933113-73-9	$16.95
Trouble with Murder, The by Kate Sweeney	ISBN: 978-1-933113-85-2	$16.95
Value of Valor, The by Lynn Ames	ISBN: 978-1-933113-46-3	$16.95
War Between the Hearts, The by Nann Dunne	ISBN: 978-1-933113-27-2	$16.95
With Every Breath by Alex Alexander	ISBN: 978-1-933113-39-5	$15.25

You can purchase other Intaglio
Publications books online at
www.bellabooks.com, www.scp-inc.biz, or at
your local book store.

Published by
Intaglio Publications
Walker, LA

Visit us on the web
www.intagliopub.com